I close my eyes and imagine the summer I discover who I used to be, who I still could be, with nobody watching. The summer I write the songs I'm meant to write, songs that are more than just starry-eyed sagas or recycled broken-heart ballads. The summer I turn down all the noise and listen to the voice in the quiet, the voice I heard when I was a little girl, telling me to stop worrying so much about what everyone else was thinking. *Close your eyes*, the voice said.

Close your eyes and sing.

Sing

Vivi Greene

HARPER TEEN

An Imprint of HarperCollinsPublishers

This book is a work of fiction. Names, characters, places, and incidents are either the product of the author's imagination or are used fictitiously, and any resemblance to actual persons, living or dead, business establishments, events, or locales is entirely coincidental.

HarperTeen is an imprint of HarperCollins Publishers.

Sing

Copyright © 2016 by Alloy Entertainment and Vivi Greene
All rights reserved. Printed in the United States of America.
No part of this book may be used or reproduced in any manner whatsoever without written permission except in the case of brief quotations embodied in critical articles and reviews. For information address HarperCollins Children's Books, a division of HarperCollins Publishers, 195 Broadway, New York, NY 10007.
www.epicreads.com

Produced by Alloy Entertainment
1325 Avenue of the Americas
New York, NY 10019
www.alloyentertainment.com

ISBN 978-0-06-245984-8

Typography by Liz Dresner

17 18 19 20 21   CG/LSCH   10 9 8 7 6 5 4 3 2 1

❖

First paperback edition, 2017

For the fans

1

THE NIGHT I get my heart broken for the last time, it's
over a bowl of soup.

The restaurant, some hip Nolita spot Jed has chosen—I
would've been happy with takeout—is packed and the
waitress tucks us into a cozy corner beneath a giant poster
of Audrey Hepburn on the back of a scooter whizzing
past the Colosseum. Jed is uncharacteristically quiet, but
he's leaving in the morning for three weeks of sold-out
shows, so I chalk it up to stress.

Until he orders the soup.

Not soup as a starter, not soup-and-something-else,
not a hearty soup, even, like bouillabaisse or bisque. Just
a mug-size bowl of minestrone that, when it arrives, turns

out to be tomato juice garnished with a few confused carrots.

This is *Jed Monroe* we're talking about. The same Jed Monroe who eats an entire stack of pancakes when I make them for breakfast every time he's in town. The same Jed Monroe who has "two dozen Krispy Kreme doughnuts (or similar)" on his tour rider and who polishes off an entire bag of mint Milano cookies in one sitting. The first time we were photographed together, the caption read something like "Beauty and the BFG." Everything about Jed is oversize, most of all his appetite, so the soup is definitely alarming. Which is why I spend the rest of the meal trying to decide if he isn't eating because he's anxious, or because he wants to fast-forward his way through dinner.

When we leave, I can feel the strained, nervous energy in his grip as he grabs for my hand, gamely smiling for fans between iPhone flashes outside the restaurant, and for the duration of the relentlessly quiet car ride home.

"I think we should talk," Jed says as we ease into a spot across the street from my building. As if on cue, the privacy window slides slowly up. The driver's blue eyes look disappointed in the rearview mirror before vanishing behind the clouded glass.

"Talk?" I try to keep the hurt out of my voice. I want to remind him that *I've* been talking all night. *He* was the one sulking into his *soup*. But I don't. I take a breath, and I smile. "Sure," I say. "Let's talk."

Jed stares at his reflection in the window, his perfectly pouty lips twisting to one side. I remember the night we met a year ago, at a party at my manager's Brooklyn loft. Terry swore he wasn't trying to set us up, but to this day I have no idea why Jed was there. *I* didn't even want to be there. Sammy had dragged me out on a pity mission less than a week after we moved to New York from LA, after Caleb and I had finally called it quits. I was hovering near the sashimi bar, swearing to anyone who would listen that I'd never date another famous person again.

But then I saw him.

Jed was alone on the balcony, staring out at the city lights like they were blinking a code he was trying to decipher. His large frame was hunched over the railing, dark against the twinkling bridge. Right away, something about him seemed different, like he was above the party and its meaningless chaos, the empty small talk, the industry pressures to always be searching for the Next Big Thing. Sure, he'd been on the cover of *Rolling Stone* just a few weeks before, but something about him appeared almost . . . normal.

I knew I shouldn't go out there. I knew I should stay inside, where it was warm and safe. Where I would be immune to the flop of his hair as it brushed across his forehead. The shy, crooked tilt of his smile. But I didn't stay. I went outside and fell in love. Again.

Big mistake.

"I don't think this is working anymore," Jed says now. He says some other things I've heard before, too, about "timing," his "priorities," his "career."

I stare into his amber eyes. I know he's in there somewhere, the one person I thought truly understood me. Understood this life, and how we'd get through it together. Jed is the first *man* I've dated. Caleb, Sebastian—they were boys. Jed's older than they were, older than me, but it's more than that. Being with him is so easy, because there aren't any games. He knows what he wants, and he knows how to get it. I just never thought he'd stop wanting *me*.

"It's . . . it's a lot of pressure," he tells me, his eyes suddenly hard and focused. "My fans are crazy. Your fans are *really* crazy."

A sick, hollow feeling sweeps over me. "My *fans*?" The one thing Jed and I always agreed on is that our fans come first. They are the reason we get to do what we do, and if that makes it harder for us to buy our own groceries, or take a leisurely walk in the park, or have a quiet dinner out, that's the price we pay. It makes having a relationship harder, but we've found a balance between going out and staying in, being accessible while still living our lives. It's not always easy, but it's worked. At least, it's worked for me.

Jed rubs the sides of his forehead, a telltale sign that he's feeling run-down. I try to convince myself that he's just tired, that all he needs is a good night's sleep. But I know Jed. Once he's made up his mind about something, there's no turning back. "I thought I could do it, but I can't," he says.

There's a lump in my throat and I want to scream at him: *Why are you giving up? We can have all of it!* But a part of me, the part I try to keep hidden, knows he's right. After all, we chose this. We get to make music and sing our songs and live our lives in front of millions of people. We don't get to be normal.

I'm just the fool who keeps trying.

Jed holds my gaze and for a moment I see something flicker in his eyes: regret, maybe, or disappointment. But he quickly looks away, digging in the pocket of his thoughtfully distressed jeans and slipping the keys to my apartment into my palm.

There are three keys: a thick, magnetic one for the front door; one for the elevator; and one for the private stairs to the rooftop deck. They're on an I ♥ NY keychain—a gift from Tess when I moved to the city—and when I think about how many times I've done this, handed over my heart, the keys to my home, to my world, I feel dizzy.

Over and over again—it's not enough. I'm not enough. The keys come back, warm from somebody else's pocket, and I'll stash them in the end table drawer, with the stray bobby pins and spare batteries and other orphaned objects, until I'm able to forget just how much this hurts. Until the next party when I can convince myself that it's worth it to keep trying. To step out onto yet another balcony, where the next guy is waiting, and start all over again.

I slip out of Jed's car in heartbroken silence, slam the door behind me, and watch his red brake lights bleed into the sea of cabs and limos on Hudson Street. I lean against my building, eyes still locked on the road. For a moment, I feel like I'm dreaming, like the real me is still in the car beside him. We're on our way back to his apartment. We're playing Ping-Pong and talking through his set list for tour. We're pulling up our schedules and figuring out when we'll be in the same city next, laughing about how crazy our lives are, how insanely difficult it can be to arrange the same nights off. We're nestled together in his king-size bed, arguing over which bad reality show to watch while we—finally—fall asleep.

I climb the steps to my front door, waiting for the tears to spill over. But they don't. It's like something inside me has shifted, and all I feel is numb. Usually I'd be rushing upstairs, ready to mess around on my guitar and scribble into my journal. The louder songs would pour out first, in fits and angry starts, and then the melancholy ballads, and finally, the full-circle, girl-power anthems. I'd have an album's worth of material jotted on napkins and notepads in less than a week, the quick-and-dirty chronicle of my latest doomed affair, from meet cute to up-in-flames to I'm-better-off-without-you.

Repeat.

I can already hear Sammy and Tess insisting that it's not me. It's him. But this time, I'm not so sure. Every relationship I've ever been in—from the big, sweeping romances that have spanned years and states to the little flirtations that were shorter but no less intense—has had two things in common:

1. The fact that they've ended, and
2. Me.

There are only so many songs a girl can write about being better off alone before she starts to believe she has no other choice.

I turn the spare keys in the lock and wedge the heavy front door open. It clicks shut behind me and I cross the lobby to the trash chute, chucking the keys inside. They clank along the sides and I wait for the satisfying sound of a final *thud*. But all I hear is quiet—quiet, and the bored, steady hum of the city that doesn't care how many times you fall apart.

2

92 Days Until Tour
June 12th

"HE'S AN ASS."

Tess arrives bearing Jeni's ice cream sandwiches and a flimsy book of matches from the bodega on the corner. We're on the roof deck, overlooking the lamplit West Village cobblestones and the dark, reflective sheen of the Hudson River.

"A giant, hairy ass," Sammy agrees. She's sprawled across one of the chaise longues, her long strawberry-blond hair fanned out behind her. Mom picked the patio furniture on one of her visits last fall, before I'd officially moved in. Neither of us had any idea that "patio" meant something different in New York than it did in Los Angeles. Or back home in Wisconsin, for that matter.

It's almost impossible to squeeze past the matching glass tables and rustic lanterns and stocky potted ferns without tripping.

"I mean, not that his ass is hairy," Sammy clarifies. "Though it probably is. I just meant that his hair is big." Between her knees is a shoebox full of cards, photographs, and other Jed-related memorabilia. She flips through a small photo book I'd had printed for Valentine's Day. "Not big. Gigantic."

Tess kicks Sammy from her post on one of the cushioned benches that line the perimeter of the deck.

"What?" Sammy whines, rubbing the side of her ankle. "It's not a secret that his hair is huge. There could be an entire colony of small creatures reproducing in there and we'd never have a clue."

I laugh, even though I don't feel like it, which is why Sammy has been my best friend since preschool. She will do or say anything to make me smile, even if it means making herself look bad, which—given her insanely long legs, porcelain skin, and freakishly shiny hair—is nearly impossible to do.

"I'm just not sure we've entered the trash-talking portion of the evening yet," Tess says flatly. She fiddles with the piercing in the soft cartilage of her upper ear, a tiny silver barbell. "We still don't even know what happened."

"I told you what happened." I groan, pulling my favorite gray cashmere sweater across my bare knees. It was the first nice thing I bought for myself when I signed to my label in LA Sammy helped me pick it out in a boutique in Santa Monica, and even though the sleeves are stretched and it's worn around the collar, I've kept it with me ever since.

"I refuse to believe you broke up with Jed Monroe because he ordered soup," Sam says. "But even if you did, I'm sure he deserved it. I mean, look at these." She pulls out a strip of photo booth shots we took at a meet-and-greet with fans a few months back. I'm making all sorts of wacky faces and Jed is pouting, his big, handsome features arranged stoically and identically from shot to shot. "Would it kill him to smile?"

I sigh. "I didn't break up with him. Stop trying to make me feel better."

Tess and Sammy exchange what is supposed to be an undercover look of concern. "Sorry." Sam shrugs. She puts the photos back in the shoebox and lays the matches beside them.

"Don't be sorry!" Tess barks. She stands abruptly, gathering her brown hair into a knot on the top of her head, exposing a newly shorn undercut that makes her look part punk, part little boy. Tess is pretty fierce about breakups, not that she's had many of her own. When she told us she was gay the summer after high school, I was relieved, figuring she'd finally start opening up about the girls she was seeing. But she didn't. As far as I know, she's never had a relationship longer than a few months. Independence is her calling card, sort of the way falling in love is mine.

I shake my head stubbornly. "I don't want to keep doing this."

"Then let's go out!" Sammy says, bolting upright. *Let's go out* is pretty much Sammy's mantra. If they gave out advanced degrees for partying your problems away, she would have her PhD.

"No," I say. "I mean, *this*." I wave distractedly at the shoebox. "I don't want to keep doing this to myself. Getting dumped, and pretending to be better for it. Writing songs about how much stronger I am on my own. Because what if the truth is that there's something wrong with me? What if I'm destined to be alone?" I bite at the corners of my thumbnail, my oldest and grossest habit.

"That's ridiculous," Tess says. "The only thing wrong with you is that you have terrible taste in men."

I roll my eyes. "You loved Jed," I remind her. "You said he was so much better than—and I quote—'the industry douchebags' I usually fall for."

Tess scoffs. "Hardly a glowing recommendation,"

she jokes, before turning serious. "No, you're right. Jed's a solid guy and a kick-ass musician. You guys, your careers . . . it all made sense. But you deserve more than a business partner. You deserve somebody who gets the real you—crazy, silly, goofy you. That's what you're looking for. Right?"

I shake my head. "I don't know," I say, stretching out my legs and looking up at the starless sky. "All I know is that I'm tired of my own battle cry. It's boring."

"Your battle cry is Billboard platinum." Sammy laughs, collapsing back onto the chaise. "You can't give up now. "

Tess kicks her again and rolls her eyes. "That's not what she means, Samantha."

"I don't know what I mean," I say with a frustrated sigh.

"I have an idea." Tess shifts closer to me on the bench. "Let's get out of here."

Sammy reaches down to pull on her sandals.

"No, no, I don't mean now." Tess raises her thick, dark brows. "For the summer."

"The summer?" Sam looks confused. "Like, the whole summer?"

I shake my head defiantly. "I don't want to go back to LA. Every time I leave the house it's like a graveyard of zombie exes."

"I didn't say anything about LA." Tess flashes a sly smile. "Remember that house my dad used to rent, up in Maine?"

I nod. Sammy and I met Tess when we were twelve, at a summer camp on Lake Michigan. Every year, after camp, Tess's father would take her back east, to a ramshackle cottage on a tiny island in Penobscot Bay. "What about it?"

"Oh, not much." Tess shrugs playfully. "Other than I just bought it."

"You *what*?" Sammy shrieks.

"You bought it?" I ask. "You didn't tell me you were thinking about buying a house!"

Tess smirks. "Just because you pay me an ungodly sum of money to hang out with you doesn't mean I have to consult you on every business decision I make," she says.

My cheeks burn. Technically, Tess and Sammy are my assistants—it's how we could justify them putting their lives on hold to keep up with mine. Sammy did a few semesters at Madison before dropping out to follow me, first to LA and then cross-country to New York. Tess was already at NYU when we got here, but it wasn't long before she decided to take a hiatus. They both insist they wouldn't have it any other way, and I know I couldn't do it without them. But I hate when they talk about money—mine or theirs—even when I know they're joking.

"It's nothing fancy," Tess continues, "just a tiny house in a real-life fishing village. I think maybe we could all use some real life for a change." Tess looks at me, and I wonder for the billionth time when she got so good at reading my mind. "What do you think, Bird? Are you in?"

Bird, originally Songbird and sometimes Birdie, is the nickname Tess gave me at camp when we were kids. Over the years it has been adapted as an easy shorthand among family and friends, to differentiate from the *other* Lily Ross, the Lily Ross who headlines tours and cranks out albums and is forever at the center of a media cyclone and who, increasingly, has almost nothing to do with me.

I stand and lean against the roof ledge, looking out over the city. A police siren pierces the air and I feel my whole body tensing. There is nothing I would love more than to leave, to hide in some cozy corner of the world, away from photographers and interviews and studio schedules. All of it.

"It's a nice idea," I say wistfully. But I know this feeling, and I know it won't last. Tomorrow it will be right back to business—there's an album to finish, the first singles to put out, endless publicity, and in the fall, my next tour. There isn't any time to feel sorry for myself.

"But . . ." Sammy prompts.

I smile. "You know I can't take that much time away from work."

Tess stares at me with her arms crossed. Sammy pretends to inspect her freshly painted, pale pink nails.

"What?" I prod. They both look like they want to say more, but don't.

"It's no big deal," Tess finally huffs, waving her hand in the air between us. "We can stay." She unpeels the wrapper from an ice cream sandwich and licks slowly around the dripping edges. "Summer in the city is delightful."

I look out at the puzzle of inching cars and shuffling pedestrians. I moved to New York because I thought it would be a fresh start. After Caleb, LA was feeling claustrophobic, like it already knew me too well. I loved the way New York made me feel off-balance. I wanted the city to swallow me up, to consume me. And it did, for about a week.

Then I met Jed. I wasn't looking for another relationship so soon, but it was almost a foregone conclusion. Our lives fit so perfectly together. We were so alike. And everything he was, I wanted to be. Successful, established, respected, grown-up. Right away, people loved us together. We were supposed to make it.

I wasn't supposed to be here, again.

Suddenly, there's an overwhelming rumbling in my chest. I turn on my heel and walk to Sammy's chaise, standing over the shoebox. I hold out one hand and without saying a word, Tess is there with the matches. I strike one and Sam passes me the photo booth strip. I tilt the flame until it licks the photo's glossy edge.

"It was fun, but now it's done," I say, the silly rhyme I stole from Sammy, the one she used to chant to get over high school breakups, back before I had any boyfriends of my own. I hold on to the burning photo, watching as Jed's face contorts, melting into mine, until the whole thing goes up in an orange burst of flame.

3

RAY IS WAITING beside one of two black Escalades parked at the back entrance of Equinox. Despite the urge to stay cocooned in my bed for weeks on end, I dragged myself to my so-early-it-should-be-illegal private session with Leon this morning, intense interval training that consistently liquefies the lower half of my body. It was typically brutal, but it felt good to be distracted, and as I approach the car I even manage something that resembles a smile.

"Nice guns," Ray teases. I lift the sleeve of my retro silk blouse to flex my wiry muscles, our post-gym comedy routine. Of the entire security team, Ray has been around the longest and is my favorite. He's sort of like an older brother, if your older brother were an ex-Navy SEAL with biceps the size of watermelons. He holds the door open and I climb in, tossing my tote on the seat beside me.

"Hey, K2." I nod at Kevin, the same driver I've had since moving to New York. Ray has another Kevin on the security team, so now we call this one K2.

"M'lady." K2 fake-bows. Even though he's from the Bronx, he has a habit of slipping into a phony British accent and calling my apartment "The Manor."

My phone buzzes and I look down to see an e-mail from Terry. The studio time has officially been booked for this afternoon. I wince. I'm supposed to be putting the final touches on my new album. But that was before yesterday, before the breakup. Now the idea of spending time with those songs, songs I've been working on for the last six months, seems impossible. Twelve songs, each one about Jed, my missing puzzle piece, all my dreams come true.

The album is titled, unbelievably, *Forever*.

"I need a fix," I tell K2, code for *If there isn't a cup of coffee in my immediate future, we'll be approaching DEFCON red.*

K2 nods and seamlessly navigates the chaos of the road. I watch his eyes flicker in the mirror, searching for the nearest Starbucks. I catch a glimpse of my own reflection. It's not as bad as I'd imagined, but there are shallow dark circles under my eyes, and my skin looks dry and dull, despite the full face of makeup I applied after getting out of the gym shower. I look like somebody who hasn't slept, which, aside from a few, fitful hours full of punishing dreams—dreams about Jed, about us together, as if nothing had happened—is true.

I tuck my phone back in my bag as K2 wedges us into an illegal spot on Thirty-third Street. Ray hops out to the curb and for a moment I consider sending him in with my order. I just don't know if I have it in me to pull it together for my fans. But getting my own coffee is a thing I do, a deal I made with myself when my world started to really change, when I started hearing my own voice on every radio station: *Don't stop doing normal things.*

I'm fully aware that being trailed by bodyguards and getting mobbed at every stop is nowhere in the neighborhood of normal, but for some reason it feels better than the alternative. No matter how surreal everything else gets, it's important to believe I can still do things for myself, even if it takes an absurdly long time to do them.

I slide out after Ray and we walk into the coffee shop together. Behind us, the rest of the security team is assembling, a handful of beefy guys in sunglasses trying to blend in with the hordes of pedestrians swarming the midtown sidewalk.

Ray holds the door open and I duck inside. As always, there are a few quiet moments before the phones start flashing and the crowd descends. Sometimes, I like to imagine that I can live in these moments. Freeze them and drag them out. Today, I use them to take a few steadying breaths. I make sure that all traces of sadness are buried deep beneath an easy, carefree facade.

As I start toward the back of the line, a trio of squealing girls shuffles over from the window. Their moms follow, iPhones at the ready, and I smile and ask their names. One of them is wearing a T-shirt that says GREELEY GYMNASTICS and I tell her I used to dream of going to the Olympics. "Now I can't do a cartwheel," I admit, and they giggle. Their moms gently guide them away after we've selfied in a variety of formations, and I inch my way closer to the counter.

Twenty minutes, twelve photo ops, and half an iced Americano later, I give Ray the sign—a tug on one earring—and a path is cleared toward the door. I've almost made it out of the frosty AC and into the sticky city heat when a girl, maybe college-age, maybe older, pops up by the counter and yells my name.

I turn to her with a warm smile, ready to sign whatever she thrusts at me, and then I see the expensive camera in her hands. She could easily be a college student studying photography, but I recognize the focused, calculating look in her eyes. *Paparazzi.*

"Where's Jed?" she calls out, once, and then again. "Where's Jed?" By now she's practically clawing Ray's elbow to keep me in her sight.

My skin starts to prickle and I hurry toward the door, but the girl scoots around Ray, camera thrust outward. "I heard you guys broke up! Is it true? What happened to *Forever*?"

There's a pounding in my chest and the smile on my face turns stale. Confused whispers travel through the crowd and there's a subtle change in the energy around me, like the charge in the air before a storm.

I reach out for the door but somehow misjudge the distance and lean into space, my legs still weak from this morning's workout. I stumble against the corner of a trash can, and before I know it, Ray is at my elbow. But it's too late: I'm going down.

The whispers turn to frenzied panic as I splay across the linoleum floor, and I feel the crowd closing in. I shut my eyes, take a deep breath, and hear the unmistakable snap of a shutter going off. I know I should get up. I know I should laugh, make a joke about being the world's biggest klutz, but I can't. I lean into Ray's shoulder as he helps me to my feet, and keep my head down as I finally duck through the door and out onto the sidewalk, tumbling into the car.

K2 peels away from the curb. He makes a series of

quick turns and soon we're careening down the West Side Highway. I look out at the river on one side, the towering clump of high-rise buildings on the other. My breathing has started to return to normal, but I still feel trapped.

This isn't the way it was supposed to happen. Usually after a breakup, I crave contact with the outside world. Being around my fans, talking to them, feeling their energy . . . it's what gets me through. It's what inspires me to get back to writing, to mine the heartache and make it my own. To wrestle it down and wring it out: a new song, a new album, a new experience.

But now it feels like I'm the one being wrung out.

I need a change of scenery. I need to be alone. I need to hear myself think.

I take out my phone and scroll through my messages, searching for a recent group text. *Changed my mind*, I type furiously to Tess and Sammy. *Need a vacation. Who's in?*

4

"WHERE ARE WE?"

I open my eyes and stare blurrily through the backseat window. I fell asleep somewhere around Portland, Maine, when Ray and the guys in the car ahead insisted on stopping for snacks. Now Tess is turning into a long, narrow parking lot and steering us toward the ocean. It feels like we could keep driving onto the rickety dock, over the water, and straight into the pale blue horizon. *Wait until I tell Jed about this,* I think, and then instantly feel the pain of losing him again. I wish I could erase him— his name, his face, his existence—from my memory.

"We're here!" Tess announces, turning off the engine of her beloved Prius—or "the Pree" as she affectionately calls it. Tess is the only one of us who drives regularly, which is ironic given that she's also the only one who has lived in the city her entire life. The Pree was the first big purchase Tess ever made and I'm pretty sure she's more attached to it than she's ever been to an actual human being.

"We are?" Sammy looks up from her phone distractedly, taking in the sleepy dock and the deserted parking lot around us. A car door slams and I see Ray loping across the pavement, looking very fish-out-of-water in his reflective Ray-Bans, black polo, and pleated khakis. He grips the inside of the passenger-side window and peers in to see me sprawled out across the backseat. "You good?"

"Just woke up." I yawn. After years of shuttling from hotel rooms to buses to planes, I can pretty much sleep anywhere. It was hard at first, but I got the hang of it: contorting my body into compact positions, tossing a sweatshirt or hat over my face, and dozing off within seconds. I stretch and sit up, noticing a smudge of orangey powder on the collar of Ray's shirt. "Cheese puffs?" I guess.

"Crap." He sighs, patting the crumbs away with one enormous thumb.

I smile. "I'm telling Lori." Ray's wife is a nutritionist and runs a tight ship. Cheese puffs are not on the meal plan.

Ray rolls his eyes before squinting into the sun. "Where's the boat?" The island is a forty-five minute ferry ride off the coast, which at first made me anxious. What will it feel like to be stranded in the middle of the ocean, with no team of stylists, no schedule, no events?

Now it doesn't feel far enough.

"Guess it's late," Tess says, fiddling with the radio. She leaves the battery running but pushes the door open with one foot. "Gives us time to get lunch," she says and climbs out. "This place has the best chicken salad on the planet."

Sammy pockets her phone and gets out of the car, pulling her hair into a messy bun at the top of her head.

Tess nods toward a quiet café at the top of a small hill. "What do you think, Ray? Gluten-free bun? Hold the mayo?"

Ray crosses his arms over his broad chest and leans against the bumper, which dips perceptibly beneath his weight. "Coffee," he grunts. "Black."

I press my forehead against the window and look out across the water. A cluster of gulls hovers above the ocean, squawking and diving in a sort of dance. I can't remember the last time I was this close to the sea. The beach was just a short drive from my house in LA, but the only time I ever spent there was the week we shot the "California Christmas" special for MTV. Otherwise, it was just the scenic blur of my daily commute to and from my house.

Choppy DJ chatter bursts from the car speakers and suddenly "You Are Here" comes on. It's a song I wrote about getting lost while driving around LA with Caleb. I still feel a little jolt every time I hear the opening bars of one of my tracks on the radio. Usually, it's a happy, heart-pumping thrill. But today it's more of a guilty pang, like I've been caught doing something I shouldn't.

Aside from my parents, I didn't tell anyone I was leaving the city. I thought about texting Terry, but I knew he'd try to talk me out of it. I've decided to call him when I get to the island, explain that getting away is the only option right now. There are three months until tour, and I have to relax before then. I can't risk another scene like yesterday. Terry won't be thrilled to hear that I've temporarily relocated to an isolated island hours and a boat ride away from any trappings of civilization, but he'll come around . . . eventually.

Out of habit, I pull my phone from the front pocket of my bag and scroll through old texts with Jed. I see my usual gushy, long-winded messages, full of kissy-face emojis and exclamation points, and his quick replies: *Yup; You too; Night*. I guess if I'd really been looking for it I would have noticed that he was distracted and curt. But why would I be looking for it? Just last week we'd done an all-day event together in Central Park. He was by my side through the whole thing, his arm hooked easily around my waist. I'd never felt so supported.

I stare off across the still water, willing the boat to appear and magically transport me to someplace where I can pretend to be somebody else.

"Welcome home!"

Tess lugs our bags out of the trunk and plops them down on the grass beside her. I peel my legs from the sticky seat and climb out of the car as Sammy bounds up to the screen door like a dopey golden retriever.

The house is small and boxy, with missing shingles and a screened-in porch that's patched with electrical tape. But the paint on the trim is new, and a cheery row of peonies lines the stone walkway to the steps.

"What do you think?" Tess asks. I follow her gaze toward the horizon. The house may be plain, but the setting is something out of a fairy tale. A thick fog snakes between clusters of giant evergreens. A low, grassy marsh opens into a web of tidal pools. And beyond all that is the ocean, flat and still and so blue it's almost black.

"It's gorgeous," I say. The air smells sweet and salty at the same time, honeysuckle mixed with gusts of a crisp sea breeze. My grandparents live in a place like this. Theirs is a lake house in Wisconsin, but the feeling of being lost in nature is the same.

"It's no Four Seasons." Tess laughs, shouldering her bag and starting for the house.

Ray leans in to scoop up my luggage, but I wave him off. "I got it," I say. "You guys go get settled. We'll call you if we make any plans."

Part of the deal I struck with my parents was that the guys had to stay at a B and B in town. I can handle being shadowed when we're out and about, but there's no way I'm spending the summer with a security team from dawn until dusk. The whole point of this trip is for me to feel normal again, and there's nothing normal about three burly bodyguards monitoring my every move.

After a thorough inspection of the house, Ray insists on rolling my bags to the steps before climbing back into his SUV and reversing down the dusty dirt road.

I open the screen door and am immediately transported to the summers of my childhood. The windows are covered in dusty plaid curtains, and there's a wood stove in the far corner of the living room. It even smells like my grandparents' house, a combination of mothballs and lingering ash from the stove.

It's perfect.

Sam and Tess are getting settled upstairs, the old

wooden floorboards groaning beneath their feet. I leave my bags near the bottom step and walk through the kitchen, a bright, narrow room with linoleum tiles and wallpaper trim. Between the kitchen and the living room is a sliding glass door that opens up to a small porch. I leave my sandals on the steps and start down the trail toward the water.

Strains of Sammy's laughter float on the breeze. I take a deep breath and feel a sharp twinge of missing home, Madison, my grandparents, and my mom and dad. I talk to them all the time, but it's not the same. It's not the same as waking up to the sounds of Mom in the kitchen, mixing batter for pancakes, classical music playing softly from the clock radio beside the stove.

Ahead of me, the water stretches out in all directions. The trail under my feet turns from rock to tall grass, opening up to a pebbly coast. I bend down to cuff the bottoms of my jeans and burrow my toes into the dark, cool sand. The waves crash into the rocks at intervals, sending up a dramatic spray of white.

My phone buzzes in my pocket and I jump. I slip it out and stare guiltily at the screen: Terry. I exhale loudly and answer the call, pressing the phone to my ear.

"Hey," I greet him, breezy and cheerful.

"Lil, what the hell?" Terry barks. "I've been texting all morning."

"I know." I sigh, backing away from the crashing surf. "I'm sorry."

"What was *that* about yesterday?" he asks. "Are you okay? I've already pulled a bunch of stuff down but a few photos got out. Did you fall? What happened?"

"I'm fine, Terry," I say. "It's just . . . Jed and I broke up. He ended it. We're through."

There's a short pause. I imagine Terry pacing the stretch of carpet in front of his desk, staring through the window of his corner office and tugging at the roots of his slicked-back hair. "I'm sorry to hear that," he says, his voice measured. "I thought you guys were—never mind, not important. What's important now is that you stay calm. Do the work, right? Nobody processes this stuff better than you do, Lil. You're the queen of bouncing back."

I slump into the sand and pick up a handful of pebbles, sifting them through my fingertips. "That's the thing," I say softly. "I don't know if I can do it this time."

"What do you mean?" Terry asks. "Of course you can. We'll put you right out there. Radio. Events. Whatever it takes to keep you busy and get ready for the fall."

I take a deep breath. "Terry. I left," I say. "I'm taking some time off."

Terry laughs. "What are you talking about? Left where?" he asks, panic creeping into his voice. "What about the tour?"

"The tour is still on," I assure him. "But I need time away. I can't . . . I need . . . I need new songs."

There's another pause, this one longer. "Terry?" I ask.

"Lily," he says, carefully, like I'm a horse he's afraid of spooking. "I understand how hard this is. Really, I do. But I think you're still in shock. *Forever* is practically in the can. It's perfect. The first single is supposed to release in a few weeks. And besides, there isn't time. You can't write, record, and promote a new album in three months."

There's a buzzing in my arms and legs, the same whirring energy I used to get whenever somebody told me I couldn't do something I wanted to do. "I don't have a choice," I say firmly. "I can't get up there and sing those songs anymore. They're lies, and I won't lie to my fans. If Jed and I are done, *Forever* is done, too."

"Lily," Terry pleads.

"I have to go," I interrupt. "I promise I won't let you down. I just . . . I need to do this. I need to do it for me. Bye, Terry."

"Lily!"

I quickly end the call and stand, wiping the sand from the back of my jeans. I take a deep breath and look out at the expanse of the ocean. The air in my lungs feels new, and the water—massive and indifferent—pulses a stubborn rhythm into my veins. It doesn't care who I am.

I close my eyes, and in an instant I feel it: coming here was, without question, the right thing to do.

The phone vibrates again inside my clenched fist. *Buzz buzz buzzzzzzzzz.*

Before I have time to change my mind, I wind up and chuck it overhead. It spins in a smooth, high arc before slipping under the still surface, swallowed into the dark, murky bay. I wait with an empty dread for the panic to set in.

But all I feel is free.

5

THE FIRST FEW days on the island are a blissful blur of lazy mornings, long lunches, and epic sunsets on the beach. A side perk of tossing my phone out to sea has been that I'm not obsessively waiting for texts from Jed . . . though of course I can't help but wonder if he's trying to get in touch. I've borrowed Tess's phone to check in with my parents, and after a few pathetic e-mails from Terry begging me to stay on top of my social media feeds, I've even posted the odd photo of my toes in the sand. But for the most part, I've managed to stay completely off the grid.

Our rhythm has already slowed to a leisurely vacation pace, though Tess insisted, over our first breakfast of granola and yogurt on the porch, that we each jot down a list of summer goals:

Tess wants to learn to surf. Yesterday morning, she rented a board from the surf shop in town and has spent the afternoon getting battered by wave after wave.

Sammy wants to read more. She picked a romance novel from the living room shelves, but so far has mostly used it as a pillow on the beach.

And I want to cook, the way I used to with Mom, before all I ate were catered meals and delivery. Something about it feels meditative, having to carefully follow so many steps. It's as if by constructing all these meals, piece by piece, I might be able to construct a better version of myself—a stronger version, one that doesn't shatter to pieces every time I end up on my own.

But what's constantly on my mind, what remains unspoken between us, is what's really on my list: to write twelve new songs by the end of the summer, a new album to replace *Forever*, that's better than *Forever*; an album I can tour with in the fall. To see myself, my music, in a different light.

So far, it's been slow going. Today I stared at the blank lines in my journal, scratching things out as quickly as I'd written them down. There's still a restless energy whirring inside me, reverberations of city life. I feel like a top that hasn't stopped spinning, as if my body hasn't quite caught up with my head.

And so it's back to the kitchen.

After we've officially overdosed on lobster rolls and clam chowder, I decide to attempt my first home-cooked dinner. Sammy and Tess hover in the kitchen, waiting for me to lose my cool. I don't. I make honey mustard chicken and coconut rice and a salad. I even toast some bread with garlic butter. There's an incident with a pan full of sizzling oil and a finicky smoke detector, but when the food is finally plated and largely resembles an actual, edible meal, I feel like a bona fide gourmand.

"This is not terrible," Tess says as we take our first bites at the round kitchen table.

"Gee, thanks," I deadpan, but I have to admit I've surprised myself. The last real meal I cooked was probably before I left home, when Mom made me help her in the kitchen on Thanksgiving. It's nice to have accomplished something, even if it's not songwriting. Anxious butterflies swarm my stomach—there are eighty-seven days until the tour, which sounds like a lot, but I can feel the hours ticking down already.

"Who wants to go out?" Sammy asks, stacking the dirty dishes after we've finished.

"Out?" Tess laughs. "Did you maybe get a little too much sun today? We're on an island with three restaurants, one of which is also the post office. There is no *out*."

Sammy drops the plates in the sink with a clatter, and I notice the pink lines of a burn on her neck. I feel suddenly guilty for dragging her here, where her fair skin and freckles will be at constant risk of sun damage, and where there isn't a decent cocktail menu within a fifty-mile radius.

"There has to be something," I insist on Sammy's behalf. "What do people here do for fun?"

Tess leans back against the wide bay window. "You're looking at it," she says.

"No way," Sammy says, turning off the faucet. "Get dressed. If there's a jukebox in this town, I'll find it."

Energized by the possibility of stimulation, I grab Tess by the hand and pull her from the cushioned bench, shooing her toward the shower. I almost make it to the top of the stairs before I remember my journal, which I stashed in Sammy's bag after the beach.

I race back downstairs and duck into the living room. The bag is slumped against the tattered ottoman, and as I pull it up by its leather handles, a magazine slides out and into my hands.

My heart drops.

There I am, in all of my clumsy glory, sprawled out on the shellacked floor of a midtown Starbucks. One arm shields my eyes but my mouth is locked in a pained grimace. In boxy white type the headline reads: *Down on Her Luck: Lily's Alone Again.*

I'm in such a trance that it takes me a few moments to register the other tabloids that have tumbled out of the bag at my feet. I glance down and am assaulted with the same photo from different angles. More oversize type, exclamation points: *Bruised and Brokenhearted: Lily Heads to Rehab* and *Where in the World Is Lily Ross?*

"Shit." I hear a voice over my shoulder. I stare at the jumbled collection of my own startled faces. Tess rushes into the room and sweeps the pile aside with one foot. Sammy stops short in the hallway behind her.

"I'm so sorry," Sammy says. "I was trying to clean out the shelves at the grocery store. They only had a few of each . . ."

"I want to see them," I say sternly.

Sammy bends down to scoop them up but Tess puts a hand out to stop her. "No," she says stubbornly. "You don't. It's all garbage. None of it is real."

I collect the magazines myself and walk briskly up the stairs.

"Birdie!" they call after me in unison.

I shake my head. "I'm good," I say, my voice trembling. "Really. I just . . . I need a few minutes."

I close the door to my room behind me and collapse onto the bed, my pulse pounding an erratic beat inside my ears. I try to count my breaths, to close my eyes and be present, but none of the usual tricks work.

This is not the first time my face has been plastered on the cover of trashy tabloids. It comes with the territory, particularly post-breakup. After my first boyfriend in LA, Sebastian, it was a circus. Word was he was cheating with one of his backup singers. Then: *all* his backup singers.

After Caleb, I was the one who was moving on too fast. I was "heartless" and "career obsessed" for ending things and moving to New York when my second album took off and his, well, didn't. I could have set the record straight, done an interview and insisted that *he* broke up with *me*, but Terry was sure it would only make things worse. The best thing to do with this kind of press is ignore it. Days later, it's always somebody else's heartbreak, someone else's mistake—real or fabricated—staring back at the world from the checkout racks.

But this time, somehow, I'm not prepared. Being here, away from everything, it's easy to forget that the world is still chugging along. Jed is still touring, answering questions, being who his fans want him to be. I'm not. I'm nowhere. So I'm fair game.

I open the magazine on top and flip slowly to the center spread. It's all there. Our last dinner date. The stupid soup. A grainy shot of me watching Jed's car as it sped away, spare keys dangling in one hand, staring after him like an abandoned puppy.

I quickly scan the poorly written copy, quoting various "inside sources" about our relationship, how it had been stalled for months. "Lily is ready to settle down, and Jed isn't. The pressure became too much."

I scoff. *Pressure?* The only thing I ever pressured him to do was sleep in on Sundays and eat fewer carbs. Tess was right. There's not a single kernel of truth to be found anywhere.

But as my eyes travel down the page, they land on a quote that makes my stomach drop. "Sources say that Lily's new album, *Forever*, was a promise to Jed. A promise he wasn't ready to make. 'It was never the big, epic romance everyone wanted it to be,' says one inside source. 'Maybe Lily thought they were *Forever*, but Jed never saw it that way. Just last month she wanted him to fly home to meet her family. He pretended he was busy with work, but really he thought things were moving too fast."

My heart feels like it's being squeezed in a vise. It was my grandparents' fiftieth wedding anniversary. My parents had planned a surprise party at the Italian restaurant where Grandpa had proposed. Jed promised he'd come, but at the last minute a bunch of appearances were added to his schedule. I hadn't told anyone he was coming. He had a habit of double-booking himself, and I was tired of getting everyone's hopes up.

There's a timid knock at the door. Without waiting for an answer, Tess and Sammy shuffle carefully into the room. "Are you okay?"

Sammy slumps beside me and rests her head on my shoulder.

"He talked to them," I say, my voice a trembling whisper. "He had to. There are things in there . . ."

"We know," Tess says quietly. "We're so sorry."

"How could he do this?" I'm genuinely bewildered. I've been around long enough to know there's no such thing as an "inside source." He talked to the press about me, my family. And *why*? So he could have the last word in our relationship? So he could come out on top? If he wanted to make me look pathetic, it worked. Tears burn my eyes and I fight not to let them spill over. If I felt shock and heartbreak when he broke it off, this is a thousand times worse—now I feel like a fool.

"You have to forget him," Tess urges. "I mean it. This is exactly why we're here."

Sammy rubs my back. "She's right," she says. "It's not worth it. This summer is for you. For us, right? Remember how fun it was, just the three of us at camp?"

"No bugs or bad food," Tess cuts in. "But otherwise, this summer should be like a grown-up version of the way things used to be. No responsibilities. No stress. Deal?"

I wipe my eyes and smile. "Deal."

"Good," Sammy says. "Now . . ."

"*Let's go out*, we know," Tess singsongs, finishing her thought. "Hold your horses, party girl. I haven't even showered."

Tess scoops up the magazines on her way out and stuffs them under one arm. Sammy lingers in the doorway. "See you downstairs?"

I shake my head and put on a smile. "You guys go ahead," I say. "I think I'll do some writing."

"No wallowing!" Tess calls from the hallway.

"No wallowing," I promise.

Sammy looks skeptical but blows me a kiss from the door.

I grab my journal from the nightstand, my guitar from its case on the floor, and cozy up in a corner of the bed, wedging the pillows behind me.

There's so much I want to say. I could write a dozen songs in the next three hours about all the ways Jed has hurt me. But they would still be about *him*. Every time I write a song it feels like I'm giving little bits of myself away. And I don't want to give Jed—or any of the guys I've dated—another piece of me.

A cool breeze tickles the back of my neck. I look out the window, where the sun has just set, casting an orangey-pink light over the treetops. The water sparkles beyond the jetties, the ocean reaching out in every direction, as far as I can see. This is why I'm here. Real quiet. Real life. Real time with real people who love me, who care about me enough to buy all ten copies of the junkiest magazines on the newsstand, just so I won't see them.

This new album needs to be different. There has to be more to me than just a girlfriend, a lonely left-behind. Before Sebastian, before LA, I'd never been in a relationship. I made it nineteen years on my own, nineteen years that I spent binge-watching *The O.C.* with Sammy, daydreaming about moving to California. Or spilling secrets to my journal on a Friday night, about how lonely it felt to be different, to never know how to say or wear the right thing. Those secrets turned into songs, my very first songs—the songs that got me a manager, a record deal, a life beyond my wildest dreams.

I close my eyes and imagine the summer I discover who I used to be, who I still could be, with nobody watching. The summer I write the songs I'm meant to write, songs that are more than just starry-eyed sagas or recycled broken-heart ballads. The summer I turn down all the noise and listen to the voice in the quiet, the voice I heard when I was a little girl, telling me to stop worrying so much about what everyone else was thinking. *Close your eyes*, the voice said.

Close your eyes and sing.

6

86 Days Until Tour
June 18th

THE CAR BLINKS and beeps and I stare at the dashboard like it's the operating system of a spaceship. The last car I drove myself was the beat-up truck my grandfather gave me when I left Wisconsin for LA There were no tricks to getting it to start, aside from revving the engine and praying a lot until it caught. The Prius has an On/Off button that should be fairly self-explanatory but somehow isn't.

Finally, with my foot on the brake, the keys in the ignition, a press of the button, and a whispered prayer, the Pree purrs to life. I glance quickly at the upstairs windows as I slowly back out of the driveway. I left a note for Tess and Sam on the fridge, but they were out late, and I doubt they'll be rallying anytime soon.

I woke up craving eggs and bacon. And pancakes. So far, Sammy and Tess have gotten all the groceries at a market in town, and I'm hoping I'll be able to find it on my own. The car bumps and lurches along the winding dirt road, feathery branches scraping at the window.

I expected to feel worse this morning. Last night, after the girls went out, I sat on the back deck for hours, watching the stars blink on and thinking more about my album. I was getting nowhere and gave up around midnight, stumbling upstairs to my room and collapsing onto the creaky twin bed. I slept hard and woke up seven hours later, in the same position, fresh and rested and ready to go. Even my body felt different, as if my bones had been shifted, my muscles stretched and realigned until all the usual touring-and-traveling aches and pains were gone.

The dirt road forks off and I turn onto pavement. The trees are thicker here and the houses closer to one another and the road. There's a small schoolhouse, and a church, and a convenience store with a single red gas pump out back. Across from the harbor is a long, low building with a swinging sign, MCCONNELL'S FOOD AND SUNDRIES.

I park and collect my bags from the front seat. There was a stash of canvas totes in the hallway closet, branded with logos from farms, the library, a bank. I grabbed a handful, along with a baseball cap I found hanging on a hook—faded blue with the red outline of a lobster. Now I pull my hair through the back of the cap and settle the hat low on my forehead. I dig around for my favorite comically oversize sunglasses and ease them on. The hat-and-shades routine hardly ever works anymore, but I still try.

I decide to make a list and I reach into my pocket for my phone, only to remember that I chucked it into the ocean. This morning, in a frenzied panic, I had snuck into Tess's room and sent a quick text to Terry asking him to FedEx me a new one. Now that I've seen the tabloids, I feel disarmingly disconnected. It was a jarring reminder that even though Lily Ross the person is on vacation, Lily Ross the business is still chugging along. On a typical day, by the time I've been awake for an hour, I've grown numb to the endless beeping of alerts, texts, and e-mails. I've also talked to Terry ten times, my parents twice. No wonder I feel so clearheaded, I realize. I haven't spent this much time alone in years.

In the market, I settle on a quick list of ingredients and begin to make my rounds. At the deli counter is a pair of girls in denim shorts, maybe nine or ten years old. They're daring each other to do something, their eyes glancing furtively at the ice cream freezers. I stand behind them, knowing what will happen when they turn around. I brace myself for squeals, iPhones, maybe even questions about the magazines and Jed.

But the strangest thing happens. The girls look up at me and I smile. They freeze. Before I can say hello, they're gone, giggling and scampering down the aisles and out through the chiming front door. I'm not sure if they recognized me or were simply scared that they'd been caught.

At the register, I wait behind a handsome young dad, his three little kids clamoring for more treats and hanging off the cart. He's so preoccupied with them that he doesn't glance in my direction. Then the middle-aged woman behind the counter swipes my card without noticing my name. I leave the store laughing, lugging the bags over my shoulder, and when my sunglasses slip off my nose, I don't even put them back on.

"What the hell were you thinking?"

The screech of tires is still ringing in my ears as I gingerly climb from the front seat. There's a puff of steam coming from underneath the hood of the Prius and my fingers are trembling. One minute, I was cruising through an intersection, almost home, windows down with the smell of the ocean filling up the car. The next, I was careening toward the passenger door of a pickup truck, slamming on the brakes too late and whipping against the steering wheel.

Tess is going to actually kill me. Her precious Pree, practically her third best friend, is wedged beneath the bed of a rusty old truck. The truck's driver is angrily prying open his door and also appears ready to actually kill me. So at least when Tess finds me, I'll already be dead.

"I'm sorry," I say. "I'm so sorry." I walk around to the front of the car, squinting to see and not-see at the same time. The car and the truck are locked together like pieces of a life-size puzzle, and there's some kind of ominous-looking fluid pooling between them on the ground. "I didn't see you."

"Well, that's a relief, I guess." The driver, a guy around my age in dirty shorts and a pale blue T-shirt, walks to the back of his truck, surveying the wreckage. "If you'd seen me or that stop sign you just blew through, I'd say you might need more than a new prescription."

It takes me a long moment to realize he's talking about my sunglasses, which I'd stashed on the top of my hat. "Oh." I pull off the glasses and wave them. "These? They're not prescription."

We're in the middle of an intersection, which, I now see, is a four-way stop. Another car, some kind of old-model Subaru, creeps up behind us, and the guy waves the driver on. Then he crouches between our cars, peering up at the underside of his truck, before glancing down at the puddle.

"They're actually just sunglasses," I explain, now wiping my lenses on the front pocket of my overalls, as if that might help. "For the sun? I got them from a street vendor in Rome."

I hear myself still talking and want to climb under the smoking hood and stay there until he drives away or I melt, whichever happens fastest. *Sunglasses? For the sun?* It's embarrassing to admit, but there are times when it's easier to be recognized. Times like these, for example, when it would give me an excuse to stop talking, or at least start talking about something else.

"You don't say," the guy grumbles from the other side of the hood. He stands and scratches his upper arm, revealing a hint of one tanned tricep. I feel my face going red, which is annoying—I'm not in the mood for muscles and blushing. I glance away from him and up at the bed of his truck. It's stacked high with long wire crates, tangles of mesh nets, and a pile of oblong buoys. Tucked between two empty traps is a long yellow surfboard, its rounded nose jutting out over the tailgate.

"You surf?" I ask as he stands, waving off the steam and lightly pressing on the bumper. "I mean, obviously. I took a lesson once. My friend wants to learn this summer. It's on her summer bucket list. Not that she's dying. She just . . . it's something she wants to do."

The guy is still carefully inspecting the hood of my car, which has finally stopped smoking. There's a gnarly looking dent in the bumper and a pattern of scratches near the front, and I'm reminded of Tess and the whole killing-me scenario, which, given the way this conversation is going, now seems like a welcome alternative.

He holds out his hand and it takes me a minute to understand that he's asking for my keys.

"Are you a mechanic?" I ask. I realize there's little chance he's going to drive off with Tess's car, and if he did, he wouldn't get far, considering we're on an island. But it still seems important to establish his credibility before handing over her keys to a complete stranger.

He stares at me for a long moment, and I'm sure this is when it will happen. When he'll finally recognize me. But I can tell by the look in his eyes—which, unfortunately, are a bright and almost breathtaking blue—that he has no clue who I am.

"No, I'm not a mechanic," he says, impatiently running a hand over the top of his cropped light hair. "Are you?"

I drop the keys in his palm and watch as he climbs into the driver's seat. "It's not my car," I call after him. "I mean, I didn't steal it or anything. It's my friend's. It's a hybrid. It's sort of tricky to turn on. There's this thing with a button?"

Within seconds the car is whirring to a frenzied start. He glances over his shoulder before slowly backing up. There's a nasty-sounding crunch as the car unsticks from the undercarriage of his truck, but he doesn't flinch. He reverses all the way back toward the stop sign, then hops out and jogs back to me.

"So what's the bad news?" I ask as he pulls open his door and starts to climb in. "How much do I owe you?"

"Me?" The guy smiles for the first time, and my insides turn to a familiar pool of wobbly goo. According to Tess, the year-round population on the island is around two thousand. What are the chances that on my first day, I literally run into the best-looking person here? "Well, it *is* a work vehicle," he says, thoughtfully tapping his fingers on the steering wheel. "Not to mention my only transportation, so . . ."

"Of course." I nod solemnly.

"I'd say about fifteen grand?" he ventures. "I mean, like I said, I'm no mechanic, but that seems a reasonable guess."

My heart clenches. Who racks up fifteen thousand dollars in damage driving on an island with four major roads and no stoplights? A boxy Jeep rolls through the intersection between us, and the driver and the guy share a wave. I duck behind my hand, imagining the next big headlines: *Lily Ross in Grief-Fueled Fender Bender.* Not exactly the "quiet escape" I had in mind.

"Fine," I huff, an embarrassed whisper. "I don't have my phone on me, so you'll have to give me your number or something . . ."

The guy looks at me for a drawn-out beat. "I was kidding," he says flatly. "Are you serious? *Fifteen grand?* This truck is older than I am. I'll probably have to *pay* somebody to get rid of it eventually."

I blink at him, flushing from the neck up. Of course he wouldn't expect me to pay thousands of dollars for a truck that looks like it's held together mostly by duct tape. I can tell by the smug lift of his golden eyebrows that he thinks I'm an absolute buffoon.

"Right," I finally manage, clearing my throat. "Of course. So . . . we're good, then?"

He smirks. "Yeah, we're good," he says, closing the door between us. The truck sputters dramatically as he turns the key in the ignition. He checks his rearview mirror and slowly pulls away, pausing after a few feet to glance quickly over his shoulder. "Just don't write a song about me or anything."

He puts on his blinker and lifts two fingers in a half wave at the mirror. I stand frozen in the intersection, a surprised smile inching across my lips, and watch as he takes the turn down another dirt road, traps and buoys and the yellow surfboard clattering in the bed behind him.

7

THE SATURDAY MORNING yoga class was Sammy's idea. She had seen a flier on the community board in the supermarket, and dragged us out of bed for it. Tess wanted to stay home—she's more inclined to beat out aggression in kickboxing than breathe it out at yoga— but after my little mishap with the Pree, she's refusing to let anybody else drive. I bet Sammy twenty bucks that Tess wouldn't last through the first sun salutation.

"Let's start with our hands on our hearts." The teacher, Maya, is around our age. She has an easy smile and seems genuine, not pretentious like a lot of the teachers I've had in New York and LA

The room is packed, a cozy attic space above the

island's only hardware store. Every so often I hear the electronic chime of the door below as it swings open, or the thud of the cash register slamming shut. I chose a spot near the wall, with Sammy to one side and an older woman in tie-dyed leggings to the other. Tess is as close as she can be to the exit.

"Let your breath be your guide," Maya says. She sits at the front of the class with her eyes closed, a thick beam of dusty sunlight caught in her long, braided hair. She is tall and toned, and dressed comfortably in a gray thermal shirt and worn, wide-legged pants.

Every so often I sneak glances at Tess, who gradually stops pouting and at one point even seems to be enjoying herself. The class feels great—calming and slow—and I make a mental note to grab a schedule on the way out.

In *savasana*, we lie on our backs. Maya sprays a lavender mist around our heads, and my limbs sink heavily into my mat. She asks us to set an intention for the rest of our day. I close my eyes and think about the people I've been watching in the mirror, the middle-aged women with frizzy hair and baggy T-shirts, a few rugged men lightheartedly grunting as they attempted to touch their toes. I wonder what their lives are like, if this is their Saturday-morning routine. Breakfast. Yoga. A trip downstairs for supplies to finish a project around the house.

There's an unpleasant fluttering in my chest—I'm jealous. There's a part of me that would give anything for every Saturday to be like this one. I know it sounds absurd, and if I ever said it out loud I'd be immediately branded as ungrateful. A lot of people—my whole family, Terry, even my friends—have made sacrifices over the years so that I could be where I am today. And "where I am today," most days, feels like on top of the world. What kind of a person would throw all that away for tie-dye and a chore list? I breathe deeply, trying to reclaim the temporary peace I'd found, but it seems I've already lost it.

There's shuffling beside me and I look up to see Sammy rolling her mat. She holds a finger to her lips and nods to Tess across the room. She's still sprawled out on the ground, and I can tell by the steady rise and fall of her chest, the heavy, outward tilt of her feet, that she's sleeping.

"Well, that sucked," Tess grumbles, her yoga mat folded sloppily under her arm.

Across the street from the yoga studio is Fresh, a vegan café. We're staring at the chalkboard menu, deciding between shots of wheatgrass and house-brewed kombucha.

"Yeah, you looked like you were really struggling,"

Sammy jokes, closing her eyes and lolling her head to one side, before breaking out in a fake snore.

"My point exactly. If I wanted to pay fifteen dollars to take a nap I could have gone to the movies. I don't need a guru for that."

Tess leans her mat against the counter and pushes in front of us to squint at the menu. As she's looking, the line shifts and I see that Maya, our serenely smiling instructor, has walked in behind us. She greets a few familiar faces and falls into line.

"Fire cider?" Tess asks, making a face. "Kombucha? Is it a requirement for there to be at least one insufferable hippie establishment within a hundred feet of every yoga studio on the planet?"

I clear my throat as Sammy looks pointedly over Tess's shoulder. "What?" Tess asks. She turns around and Maya wiggles her fingers in a teasing wave.

Tess's face, still pink from the heat of the studio, flushes an even deeper crimson. "Oh," she says. "Hey. I didn't mean . . ."

"No, it's a really good question." Maya nods, a spirited sparkle in her big green eyes. "I'll have to take it up with my *guru*."

Sammy and I laugh while Tess fidgets uncomfortably. It's not very often that she's put on the receiving end of this kind of banter, and it's entertaining to watch.

"I'm only teasing," Maya says, touching Tess lightly on the shoulder. "But you really should try the fire cider. It's life-changing."

As a peace offering, I insist on treating Maya to a cider shot, and she suggests that I get a round for the rest of us, too.

"What's in it?" Sammy asks as the barista hands over the squat glasses. She leans in and crinkles her nose at the pungent smell.

"It's vinegar infused with horseradish and a bunch of other stuff," Maya explains. "It's like a power-washing for your insides."

"And that's a good thing?" Tess asks quietly, clearly still recovering from the taste of her own foot in her mouth.

Maya smiles. "It's never a bad idea to start over," she says, holding up her shot glass. It may be something in her eye, but I swear she winks at me as we clink glasses. For a paranoid second, I wonder if she was actually reading my mind in class.

We knock back our ciders—it's like a mix between mouthwash and a Bloody Mary, in a not entirely unpleasant way—and say good-bye to Maya, promising to come back to class next weekend.

There's a small corner table in the back of the café and I duck toward it. A freckled girl with pigtails stops me on the way to ask for a photo, and I oblige. It's only happened a handful of times since we've been here, and everyone has been so polite that I haven't minded, but today, it gives me a little shock. It's been amazingly easy to forget that I'm famous. I sort of expect that everyone else has forgotten, too.

"What's up?" Tess asks, apparently reading a new shadow on my face.

"I just don't know what the point is anymore." I sigh, nibbling at the corner of my sunflower seed muffin.

"The point of what?" Sam asks.

"Why am I even trying to pretend like I can escape?" I ask. "Everyone in this room knows that I've just had my heart broken. If they're not talking about it, they're thinking about it. And we're on an island with no chain restaurants and a video rental store that still carries *actual* videos. Do you have any idea how messed up that feels?"

Sammy opens her mouth and I know she's going to say something to cheer me up, the way she always does, but I keep talking. It feels like if I don't get it all out, the way I've been feeling, the uneasy sensation in my chest might get stuck, swelling and spreading until it crushes me completely.

"I'm so sick of the drama. And I hate that everyone expects me to roll over and turn every crappy thing that happens to me into a song. What if I don't want to write about getting my heart broken for the fifteenth time? What if I don't want to write a love song at all?"

We're all quiet for a few moments, until Sammy clears her throat. "Are you saying you want to stop singing?"

"No," I huff. "I just wish I could figure out a way to write about something that isn't Jed."

"So do it," Tess says simply. She's always doing this, making me feel like I'm overcomplicating things, like if I didn't spend so much time in my head, if I could get out of my own way, everything would be so much easier. I watch her stir sugar into her coffee. I watch Sammy break her scone into tiny, uniform pieces. I feel a sudden, empty sadness. These are my best friends, the people who know me better than anyone else in the universe. If they don't understand how hard this is, how can I ever expect anyone else to?

My phone buzzes on the table. I lean over to glance at the caller ID. Tess and Sammy do, too. It's Jed.

My stomach drops, and I snatch the phone up. "Don't answer it," Sammy blurts.

It's the first time he's called since I left. The first time that I know about, anyway. I received the FedExed phone from Terry almost immediately, but I waited a day before activating it, and now I can't stop staring at it, willing every vibrating alert to mean a message from Jed. I quickly scan my memory of his schedule, wondering where he is. London? Spain? What time is it there? Is he alone?

"She's right," Tess says. "What could he possibly say that would make you feel better?"

I think about it, my fingers clutching the phone's smooth sides. Even if he says he was wrong, that he's made a mistake, he wants me back, it won't change the fact that he talked to the press and made me look like a whiny, needy, lovesick little girl.

I drop the phone and watch as it shudders across the table. It finally stops its tortuous buzzing and we wait to see if he leaves a message. The screen goes dark. He doesn't.

I swallow, my jaw clenched, a throbbing pressure behind my eyes. Every part of me wishes I could hear his voice, ask him about his shows, tell him all about the island and how much he'd love it. It's like my brain has been reprogrammed, but my body, my heart, are still stuck. Even after the way things ended, all I can think about is the way we used to be, a time—not so long ago—when my days weren't complete until I shared them with him. There's a tiny part of me that feels like this whole thing is truly just vacation, and when I get back to New York, I'll return to my old life, my old routine. And Jed.

I feel Sammy's and Tess's eyes on me as I stare at the phone. Tess pulls her own out of her pocket and checks the time. "We're late," she says quickly, heading outside as she makes a call.

I glance up at Sammy. "Late?" I ask. "Late for what?"

Sammy stands, gathering our plates. "Didn't she tell you?" she asks, glancing through the wall of windows. Outside, Tess paces a stretch of the sidewalk, smiling into the phone. "She ran into a bunch of guys she used to hang out with. They offered to take us fishing."

"Guys?" I ask suspiciously. "What guys? When?"

Sammy shrugs. "At the bar the other night. Some guys she used to play with when she was little. They seemed nice. I thought she told you." She walks briskly toward the trash.

"No, she didn't tell me," I say, hurrying to catch up. "I'm pretty sure I'd remember hearing about a post-yoga fishing date. Nice try."

Sammy smiles sheepishly. "Tess thought you wouldn't go unless we bribed you with snacks," she says, tossing the rest of my muffin into the compost bin.

I can't help but laugh. They may not understand every aspect of what I do, the impossible balance of life and career—but they know *me*. We walk outside and I stop short in front of the big window. "I haven't showered," I say, catching sight of my reflection. My hair is flat and sweaty, the straps of my halter are twisted in the back.

"I'm supposed to wear this?"

"You're the one who wants to be normal," Tess says, linking her arm in mine as she drags me toward the car.

"Hop in," she orders. "I'm driving."

84 Days Until Tour
June 20th

THE HARBOR IS busy, bustling with fishermen in orange pants and suspenders loading and unloading gear and traps from a line of bobbing boats. We park in a half-empty lot, and as we get out of the car, a brisk ocean breeze whips my hair from my face.

I shiver. "I wish I'd known you made plans," I mutter, rubbing the sides of my bare arms. "I would have worn something warmer."

Tess glances across the street at a gas station/convenience store/fisherman's supply shop. "They might have something in there."

I head inside and quickly scan the limited selection, ultimately settling on an enormous gray hooded sweatshirt, the words I GOT LUCKY AT LUCKY'S BAIT & TACKLE printed on the back. An old man with thick glasses and crooked teeth takes my card without looking at it, pushing a glass bowl of hard candies across the counter at me. I choose a butterscotch to be polite and hurry back outside.

Tess and Sammy are at the end of the dock beside a small lobster boat. The front of the boat sweeps up into a high point, and there's a wide, covered cockpit shielded by dirty windows. Two guys are busy passing empty crates onto the lowered back end.

"Where's Noel?" Tess asks as I join them.

One of the guys, heavyset with a scruffy red beard, answers without looking up. "Probably sleeping in." He laughs. "I swear, if this wasn't his old man's boat . . ." He looks up quickly, his mouth stuck in an O as he stares directly at me. "Holy shit, you're Lily Ross!" A shocked smile spreads across his face. "Latham, you're not gonna—" He's interrupted by a slap upside the back of his head. "Jesus, what was that for?"

The slapper, a smaller guy with dimples and patches of light blond scruff, climbs out of the boat, wiping his hands on his cargo shorts. He smiles at me, holding out a hand. "Sorry about him. I'm Latham. Captain Obvious over here is J.T. It's an honor to meet you. We're all really big fans. I love that one song, what's that one, about the summer . . . ?"

"That really narrows it down," says a voice behind me. Tess breaks into a smile.

"Noel!" Tess rushes across the dock and I turn. I see his truck first, old and banged-up, with a familiar dent on one side. As Tess wraps him in a hug, my eyes meet his, and the back of my neck goes hot and scratchy.

It's the guy from the intersection.

"Sammy, Bird, this is Noel," Tess says, her face lit up. "He's the only reason I survived my summers here."

Noel smiles, shaking Sammy's outstretched hand. "I don't know about that." He turns to me and his smile slowly fades. "Hello," he says gruffly.

Blood rushes to my cheeks. "Hey," I say much too loudly.

Tess looks skeptically from Noel to me. "You two know each other?"

"Not really," Noel says, pulling down the tailgate of his truck. "Wasn't much time for small talk while she was demolishing my truck."

Tess furrows her dark brow, glancing at the dent behind the door. "You did this?" she asks me. "I thought you said it was a fender bender."

Before I can make an excuse, J.T. cuts me off. "Hold

up." He laughs. "You got into a *fender bender* with Lily Ross, and this is the first we're hearing of it?"

Noel shakes his head, lugging a few crates from the truck's bed. He pushes them into J.T.'s chest. "Easy, fanboy," he teases. "We're late."

Tess and Sammy laugh as Latham helps us all into the back of the boat. "*We're* late?" J.T. is still ribbing Noel. "You're the one who took his sweet time getting over here this morning. What happened, you get rear-ended by Madonna?"

Noel flashes the easy smile of someone who could have the last word but chooses not to and lowers the last of the traps into the back of the boat.

"Everyone ready?" Noel asks. He starts the engine without waiting for an answer and we sputter away from the dock, the harbor and the town receding into the distance.

Sammy and I squeeze onto a small bench seat toward the back, the salty spray of the ocean misting our faces. J.T. and Latham are crouched over a pair of giant coolers, spearing thick slabs of bait with what look like giant barbeque skewers. Tess stands next to Noel, chatting. The roar of the engine and whoosh of the wind make it impossible to hear anything, so I just stare out at the water. The sun beats down in shimmering strokes, but the air is crisp as we pick up speed, and I'm grateful for my giant, if far-from-flattering, sweatshirt.

I haven't been on a boat like this since I was little. My grandpa used to take me fishing every summer, when we stayed at their house on the lake. There's a particular feeling you get, surrounded by water, with the sky so big and full overhead. I'd forgotten how much I'd missed it.

After a while, Noel cuts the engine and we stop at an orange buoy with two white stripes. The guys get to work, their movements a carefully choreographed routine. They pull up the buoy and hook it to a pulley that hangs off one side of the boat. A giant metal trap splashes out of the water. They swing it into the back of the boat as Sammy and Tess and I hover around the perimeter, water sloshing around our feet.

"Not bad." Latham grins, lifting the hatch. The trap is crawling with blue-black lobsters of various sizes, their prehistoric-looking claws hinging slowly open and shut. The guys toss the lobsters into giant coolers stashed beneath the benches.

As we pull up to the next buoy, Noel gestures impatiently for more bait. He peels off his rubber gloves and walks to the back of the boat, brushing past me without so much as a look. Something about his active disinterest makes me bristle. "What have you guys been doing back here?" he shouts, peering into the cooler of bait. "Daydreaming?"

J.T. starts setting the traps as Noel hurriedly slaps some more chunks of slimy flesh onto the skewers. I watch him for a moment, that same stubborn instinct bubbling up inside of me. From the time I was a kid, I've had this thing about getting people to like me. It sounds ridiculous now, but it's never gone away. Maybe it's part of the reason I've been so successful—my fans can tell I need them as much as they need me.

I head to the back and kneel down beside Noel, rolling up my sleeves. The plastic bin is full to the brim with stinky fish guts and broken pieces of crab shells. I observe him quietly for a moment, then pick up one of the long needles and dig my hands into the slippery mess.

"Mackerel?" I ask, holding up a small, silvery fish.

Noel looks down at me, over his shoulder. His eyes are even lighter than I remember, almost transparent blue, and the skin around them is soft and freckled. He blinks in surprise. "Yeah. You fish?"

"I used to," I say, piercing the fish with the sharp end of the giant needle and laying it into the trap behind us. "With my grandpa. Ice fishing, too."

I feel Noel staring as I skewer a few more pieces.

"Lily's full of surprises," Tess interjects. "You should

see her during hunting season. She's a beast with a twenty-two."

I roll my eyes as J.T. looks up from the traps. "Really?" he asks, grinning.

"No, not really," I say, baiting more fish. "That's just what I need. I can see the headlines now: *Lily Ross: Armed and Dangerous.*"

Noel laughs, a genuine chuckle, and I feel the quick thrill of success. "All right," he says, pushing up to his feet. "Drop 'em in and let's keep moving."

Latham and J.T. fill the now-empty pot with fresh bait and lower it back into the water, while Noel starts the engine and steers us to the next buoy, a few hundred yards away. We keep on like this for most of the afternoon. The guys make a game out of scaring Sammy with flailing lobsters, and J.T. shows Tess how to pull in the pots. Whenever we get low, I help Noel with the bait. He doesn't say much, but eventually he seems to relax. I wonder if he's like my grandpa, not really himself unless he's on the water.

After the sixth stop, Noel steers us back toward land. I catch his eye from my spot on the bench and he nods me over.

"Want to drive?" he asks, not looking at me.

"Me?"

"Sure." He shifts over a bit and releases the shiny

wheel. "As long as you promise not to T-bone anything. Think you can handle that?"

"I can try," I say with a laugh. He pulls the engine into gear and we jolt forward, a spray of wake kicking up alongside us. We bump over choppy swells and I squint into the sun. All around us is ocean, an endless, mirrored canvas, and suddenly I'm nine years old on a summer afternoon, with nothing to do and no one to please.

9

81 Days Until Tour
June 23rd

I'M SECONDS AWAY from drifting off to sleep when my phone buzzes on the bedside table. It's probably Terry, I think, with more bad publicity news, or an addition to the fall tour schedule I'll have to stress about. Maybe a label guy, wondering when to expect the new music. Or my mom, who still likes to check in and say good night.

Whatever it is, it can wait until morning.

Thirty seconds later: another buzz. I sigh and flip the screen over, the blue glow illuminating the dark of my small room.

Two texts from Jed: *Hi*, and then, *You there?*

A quick burst of adrenaline shoots through my veins.

I'd finally managed to stop obsessing over the last time he called. Since he didn't leave a message, I'd convinced myself that it was an accident. A pocket dial, or an awkward slip of his thumb.

But now there's proof. He finally wants to talk.

It's been eleven days. Eleven days since my life collapsed, my world turned totally upside down. It feels like yesterday and a lifetime ago, all at once.

I swipe the screen awake. My thumbs hover over the keypad. Do I answer? Right after the breakup, it would have been easy. All Jed would have needed to say was that he'd made a mistake. That he missed me and wanted things to go back to the way they were. We could wipe the slate clean, pretend that none of it had ever happened.

But now, it's different. The things he said—the things that were printed—will live on, long after the magazines have been tossed in the trash. Anytime anyone searches my name, it will all come back. We were a team, and now we're not. It's over.

I toss my phone back onto the nightstand and lean heavily into the pillows. I feel almost sick. How can somebody be two people at the same time? There's Jed, the guy on the balcony I couldn't wait to get to know, the person I imagined would be my other half *forever*. Jed, the guy who knew exactly how I was feeling, exactly what I was going through, exactly all of the time.

And then there's the other Jed, at the restaurant, playing with his soup. Jed in print, telling our secrets, betraying my trust, making me look like a fool.

I groan and throw off the covers. Sleep is definitely out of the question.

Through the window, the moon is big and ringed in gauzy white. I pull on a long cardigan over my pajamas and stuff my journal and a pen into the oversize front pocket. Maybe I can distract myself by writing. I creep downstairs and find my flip-flops and a towel.

Outside, the air smells like rain. Afternoon showers kept us inside most of the day. I had taken out my guitar for the first time since we've been here and messed around while Sammy read and Tess tried to nap. I hadn't played music just for fun in a while. Without the stress of trying to come up with a melody, it started to feel natural again.

I follow the moonlit path to the stretch of beach behind our house. It's quiet, and a little bit eerie, and I think for a minute about turning back, but there's something about the ocean that draws me in. I need to feel something big, bigger than the doubts and anxieties that live inside my head. Something powerful and self-assured.

I strip and leave my clothes and towel in a pile on the rocky shore, then splash into the ocean before I have time to change my mind. The water is brutal and exhilarating.

It shocks my limbs and turns them instantly numb. My heart feels like it's stopped beating. *Good*, I think. *Maybe if my heart is frozen, it will stop aching once and for all.* Moments or minutes later, when I feel on the verge of true hypothermia, I stumble over the rocks toward the beach.

Back on dry land, I close myself in the big, warm towel, and stare up at the glow of the moon. Ahead, the coastline stretches out for miles. I find a clear patch of sand, wiggle into my clothes, and nestle into a spot on the shore.

I lean back and close my eyes. A snatch of melody has been running through my mind since this afternoon. Sometimes it feels like songs flutter in and out of my consciousness like teasing butterflies, daring me to catch them.

I almost have the lyrics—something about morning amnesia, waking up in a strange bed and remembering, every time, that you're alone. When I open my eyes each day, I've forgotten where I am, and why I'm here. It's sort of like meeting yourself for the first time, just for a moment, before it all comes rushing back.

It's not only the fact that I'm in a strange house. For the first time in years, I'm totally and completely unattached. The last time I spent a full week on my own was when I'd recently moved to LA. In what is now essentially part of the public record, I took a waitressing job and worked all of one shift before quitting. Sebastian was at my first table. He asked for my number with the check, and we went out the next night. Three weeks after that, we moved in together.

I'm not exactly used to taking things slow.

The melody—simple, and a little bit melancholy—runs through my whole body, but as soon as I find it, it's gone again. I open my eyes and stare up at the star-studded sky, waiting for something, anything, to find me.

There's a whooshing sound in my ears. My eyes snap open, dusty sunlight blurring the horizon. What time is it? Have I been out here all night? I hear a ragged panting and feel a slobbery tongue on my cheek. I sit up in alarm, but it's quickly replaced by a pleasant surprise: there's a long-haired black-and-white dog investigating my towel.

"Hi there, handsome." I nuzzle the dog's nose and he licks me again, this time more aggressively, until I'm pinned on my back, smothered in his salty, damp fur.

"Murphy!" a voice calls from down the beach. In the dim morning light, I see the shadow of a person running, a head bobbing up and down at the water's edge. "Murphy, come!"

I'm laughing, shielding my face with my arms to ward off any further advances, when someone appears beside me.

"Murphy, enough," the guy says firmly, lugging the dog by the scruff of his neck and nudging him behind his legs. His face is turned away, but I recognize the subtle smile in his voice. Noel. "Sorry. He's usually not so forward."

I wipe the slobber from my cheek and smile. "No problem." The dog grips one of my flip-flops in his teeth and takes off toward the water.

"Murphy!" Noel groans. "Are you kidding me?"

"Let him go." I laugh. "He's having so much fun."

"You sure?" he asks. "He's probably going to sell it on eBay or something. He has pretty questionable morals."

"Yeah," I say, watching as the dog darts up and down the winding beach, waving my shoe back and forth like a giant chew toy. "He seems like a real menace."

Noel chuckles, still out of breath from running up the beach.

"Do you want to sit?" I ask. "Looked like you worked up to a full sprint there."

"That was nothing. You should see me when he steals a wallet." He settles into the sand beside me. I fiddle with the tattered seam of the towel and pull down the sleeves of my sweater. Noel stares out at the calm of the ocean, and I sneak a glance at his profile. It still seems insane, and almost cruel, that there could be somebody so spine-tinglingly good-looking on an island so remote, and that I would end up sitting beside him, alone, on a beach, at sunrise.

I try to distract myself by wondering how old he is. His blue eyes are deep and ageless, but there's something boyish about him, too. Even when he's not smiling, there's a lightness to him, like he's remembering a joke he's not yet ready to share.

"You live near here?" I ask, trying to strike a perfect balance of breezy and polite.

Noel gestures up the beach toward a cluster of houses on a hill. "Just beyond the point," he says. "There's a path. It's a bit of a hike from the water. That's where the real people live."

"Real people?"

"Year-rounders," he explains. "People from here."

"Not Tess," I clarify.

"Not Tess. Not you," he says. "You're from away."

"You can say that again," I say, hearing the wistful self-pity in my voice and wishing I could erase it. I clear my throat. "What about you? You grew up here, I know. But do you still live here all the time?"

"Every day," he says. "I left for college, but only lasted a little while. There's a lot to complain about, especially in the winter, but after growing up here, it's hard to live anywhere else."

"I can see why." I look out at the painted clouds creeping around the rising sun. "I can't remember the last time I've spent this much time outside. It's amazing how far away everything else feels. In a good way."

"It's like everything's on a different scale," he says. "Stripped down or something."

I nod. It's exactly how I've been feeling. Unencumbered. Raw. Exposed.

We're quiet again for a moment, sitting in an easy, comfortable silence. It's hard to believe this is the same guy from the car accident, the same guy from the boat. I no longer feel the insane urge to make him like me because, I realize with a jolt, he's sort of acting like he does.

"Sorry, about before," he says suddenly, as if reading my mind.

"What do you mean?" I ask innocently.

He sighs, leaning back to look me in the eyes. "I wasn't exactly the world's greatest host."

I stare at him carefully, waiting to see if he'll say more.

"Bad day?" I ask when he doesn't.

"A few of them," he says with a tentative smile. It's a smile I recognize right away: the one you try on when your face wants to be happy but the rest of you hasn't quite caught up. It's been a permanent part of my wardrobe, of late. "And when you . . . when I saw you . . ."

"You thought I was some privileged celebrity here to invade your island and screw up your summer?" I guess.

Noel runs his hand through his hair sheepishly. Adorably. "Not in so many words, but . . . something like that."

"It's okay," I say. "I understand." I look out at the ocean and watch Murphy splashing in the frothy surf. A breeze rolls off the water and I pull my sweater closer.

"Did you sleep out here?" he asks, as if noticing for the first time that my hair is full of sand.

"I guess so." I laugh. "I came out last night to go for a swim, and the next thing I knew . . ."

His eyes widen in surprise. "You went in? You're insane!"

"I am?"

"I don't swim in this water until the middle of August." Noel shakes his head. "Nobody does."

"It was refreshing," I insist. "You should try it."

Noel cocks his head as if he's trying to figure out if any of this is real. "This has got to be pretty different from the way you normally vacation, right?" he says. "Private yachts. Infinity pools. That's more your scene, I bet."

"You have me all figured out," I say. "Ibiza or bust."

He laughs, a genuine laugh that makes my cheeks warm with pride. It's been a long time since I've had to work so hard to earn a real laugh from somebody. I realize, with surprise, that I like it.

"My sister is going to lose it," he says. "I promised her the next time I hung out with you guys I'd bring her along. She's kind of obsessed."

"Really?" I smile.

"Really," he says. "It's weird. I mean, she's fourteen. But she's super smart."

"And smart people don't like my music?"

"No, I didn't mean . . ." Noel lowers his head onto his crossed forearms. "This is why I try not to talk. It usually just gets me in trouble."

"I'd like to meet her," I say. "Your sister."

"You will." Noel lifts his head back up. "She's probably hiding in the bushes right now. Or she would be, if she hasn't stayed up all night doing her homework."

"Homework?" I ask. "Isn't school out for the summer?"

"She takes classes," he says. "For *fun*. She's not normal."

"She sounds great."

"She is." Noel stares up at the blue sky and stretches his legs out toward the ocean. "She's the reason I came back."

It's clear there's more to the story, and I get a strange sensation that he wants to talk about it, but I feel like I've done enough prying for one morning. "Well, I hope you didn't tell her what a terrible driver I am," I say lightly.

"I sure did," he says. "I also told her you were a pretty solid first mate."

I sneak another glance at him, trying to fight back a smile. "I can live with that."

Noel looks at me for another long moment, like he wants to say something else. But instead of speaking, he hops up to his feet, hooks two fingers in his mouth, and whistles loudly. "Let's go, you lunatic," he calls to Murphy, who sprints toward us, my flip-flop still clenched in his jaws.

"Give the lady back her shoe," Noel orders, and amazingly, the dog obeys, dropping it onto the sand between my feet.

"Wow. You really have him trained."

"You wouldn't believe the money I spend on treats," he says. "He's got expensive taste. Only organic."

I scratch behind Murphy's ears. "It was nice to meet you," I say as the dog licks me one last time.

"The pleasure is all his," Noel says gallantly. "Glad to see you're keeping off the roads."

I hug my sweater tighter. "Strictly pedestrian," I vow.

He taps the outside of his dark jeans and starts

walking, Murphy skipping behind him to keep up. He's almost to the water when he turns around and cups his hands around his mouth. "Hey! Can I ask you something?" he calls out.

"Sure!" I yell back.

"Would you want to maybe hang out sometime?"

Before I can help myself, I'm laughing, harder than I have in a long time. Partially because it's so unexpected, and I'm not sure how else to respond, but also because I've just spent the night in the sand and a guy I barely know is yelling at me on a beach. And for some stupid, misguided, and all-too-familiar reason, I don't want him to stop. Murphy runs back and sniffs my ankles, and Noel follows.

"Sorry," he says. "I thought it might be easier that way, in case you said no."

"Okay," I say, regaining my composure and standing up at last.

"*Okay*, you want to hang out?"

"Sure," I say, even though everything rational in me knows it's the opposite of what I should be saying. The opposite of why I'm here. The last thing I need to do. "Why not?"

"Cool." He smiles, wrinkling the corners of his crystal-blue eyes. "Like, at a reasonable hour, maybe?" He points to my pajamas. "You could wear real clothes."

"I'd like that."

Noel nods, as if still convincing himself that I actually said yes. "Right. Okay. So we'll hang out."

"We'll hang out."

We stand there, sort of awkwardly nodding at each other for a second, until I remember my journal in the pocket of my sweater. "Here," I say, handing him a pen. "Write down your number."

He scribbles it sideways in the margins of a blank page. "Just, you know. Don't go passing it around," he fake-whispers. "I'm trying to keep a low profile."

"Scout's honor," I promise.

He holds up his hand in that same lazy wave and calls to Murphy again. They run back along the water toward the faraway cluster of houses. I watch as they get smaller, bobbing alongside the coastline, turning the bend and disappearing around the point. I gather my things and head back up the path, shaking my head.

Here we go again.

10

WHEN I GET home I curl up in bed, and though I'm sure it will never happen, I manage to get some more sleep. I wake up slowly a few hours later, and as the hazy memories of those early morning hours start to come back, I'm gripped by an intense game of emotional tug-of-war.

Part of me loves it—the familiar, fuzzy aftershock of meeting someone new. It feels like I've been stalling, my batteries running low, and now, after one little encounter, one glimmer of attention and interest, I've been fully recharged, my spirit shocked back to life.

On the other hand, I feel pathetic. I've never thought of myself as having an addictive personality. But now, I know the truth. I'm a love addict, and I've fallen off the wagon.

I roll over in bed and reach for my journal, flipping to the page where Noel wrote his number. I stare at the slope of the sevens, the quick, confident dashes between lines. What kind of ridiculous person gets butterflies looking at ten numbers scrawled in the margins of her notebook?

An addict. That's who.

I slap the notebook shut and pull the blankets back over my head. It's not too late, I tell myself, taking deep, controlled breaths. Just because he gave me his number doesn't mean I have to use it. There's still time to be strong.

I should probably just stay in bed.

"Ladies and ladies," Tess shouts from downstairs. "Your chariot awaits!" Tess has seemed to relish her self-appointed role as tour guide/activities director lately.

I groan out of bed and shuffle toward the door. "Now what?" I peer sleepily down the stairs.

Today, Tess is wearing a long-sleeved black shirt with a skull-and-crossbones printed across the chest, cargo pants, and hiking boots. She looks like a cross between a Girl Scout and the drummer in a heavy metal band. "We're going for a walk. There are ticks. Wear layers."

"Ticks?" Sammy calls out from her room. "No thanks."

"It wasn't a question," Tess yells. "This summer of bonding was your idea, Samantha. Now get down here and bond."

I close my door and head into the bathroom, hoping a shower will turn things around. After, I stare at my phone, considering leaving it behind. But I know it's not an option; Terry is finalizing tour dates and there are all kinds of details I'll need to approve. He'll have a panic attack if I'm not reachable all day long. There's an anxious rumble in my stomach at the thought of the tour—we've been here almost two weeks and I still haven't written a single song. I grab my journal, too. If I can just steal a few minutes this morning I might be able to get some lyrics down. It's not a whole album, but it'd be something. Terry would be so relieved . . . and, truthfully, so would I.

Sam's door is still closed when I leave my room. I knock quietly and hear some shuffling and a soft thud. Finally she calls out: "Come in!"

Sammy's spread out on her bed, a paperback novel—the same one she's been reading since we got here—propped open.

"You're really not coming?" Sam's room is tiny and toward the front of the house, the only one without a view of the ocean. When we got here it was assumed that Tess would take the cozy room in the back that she'd slept in when she was a kid, and I got the master suite at the end of the hall. I haven't spent much time in the room Sammy was left with, and I now realize that it's actually more of a storage space, with a portable wardrobe and a frameless twin bed pushed up against one corner.

"Do you mind if I hang out here?" Sammy looks at me apologetically. "I'm really into this book."

I lean over her shoulder. "What is it?"

She flops it shut. "Just some sappy love story." The cover shows a muscular man with Fabio hair embracing a woman in a flapper dress in front of an airplane hangar. "But it's really well written."

I laugh and rest my hand on Sammy's head. "I'm glad you like it." Sammy's never been much of a reader. In high school I used to help her write her papers; in exchange, she'd take me shopping and help me pick out what to wear to the open-mic nights I played in Madison.

"Want us to bring you back anything for lunch?"

"As long as it isn't a lobster roll," Sammy says, making a face. "After our little fishing trip, I don't think I can ever eat one of those poor creatures again."

I gesture toward the open window. "The sun's out again. Don't stay inside all day."

Sammy promises to at least read on the deck and I

run downstairs and out the door, where Tess and Ray are waiting with the car.

"I think Sammy has a secret."

Tess is a few feet ahead of me on the trail, her boots trampling over roots and fallen pine needles. She turns over her shoulder and gives me a doubting look.

"Our Sammy?" she asks. "Sammy has never kept a secret in her life. Remember the surprise party debacle?"

A few years back, Terry and Tess and Sam and my parents got together to throw me an epic surprise bash at Disneyland, of all places. There was an elaborate cover involving a music video shoot, and I thought we were just going to work. But the night before, Sammy let slip that the massive icebox cake she'd ordered (my favorite) would have to be picked up in the morning.

"Remember she tried to play it off?" I chuckle. "Like it was a surprise party for somebody on the crew, who also happened to have a birthday and love theme parks and icebox cakes?"

Tess laughs and stops in the middle of the trail, crossing her arms over her waist like she's fighting off a cramp. "Oh man." She sighs, catching her breath. "So what's the secret?"

"What do you mean?" I blurt. My journal and phone

are burning holes in the pocket of my sweatshirt, and I've been thinking about sneaking a text to Noel all morning.

"You said Sam has a secret," Tess reminds me, her eyebrows arched in suspicion. "Somebody's jumpy."

"Sorry," I say, pushing on through an opening in the trees. "There's just no way she cares that much about a book. She was being kind of weird this morning."

"Well, that makes two of you," Tess says, hustling to catch up.

I force a grin. "Are those blueberries?" I ask, a not-so-subtle attempt at changing the subject. Luckily, Tess is an undercover nature freak, the hidden underbelly of her city-girl status that grew out of her summers here on the island and at camp.

"Yup." Tess nods, bending down to pick the tiny, wrinkled berries. She pops a few in her mouth and hands the rest to me. They are sweet and tart at the same time, nothing like the mushy, tasteless fruit you find in stores.

"Wow," I say. "These are incredible."

"Good things come in small packages." At barely five feet tall, Tess is a sucker for anything tiny. "Come on," she urges. "We're almost to the summit."

Out of the corner of my eye I spot a wooden bench, wedged between a pair of pine trees. "Do you mind if I meet you up there? I want to write down some lyrics before I forget them."

"New song?" Tess turns around quickly, and there's a glimmer of relief in her eyes that makes my stomach clench. She and Sammy have bent over backward for me, encouraging me to take a break, to recharge, but deep down, they must be scared, too. In a lot of ways, my career is their career.

"Maybe," I say carefully, afraid to commit to too much. "I'm not sure yet."

Tess gives me an encouraging nod. "You got this, Bird."

I manage a strained smile and watch as she starts back on the trail. "See you at the top!" She calls over her shoulder, disappearing around a wooded bend.

I follow the sandy path out to the small point and sit down on the bench that overlooks the water. In the distance there is a collection of smaller islands, connected by narrow patches of marshland. Shorebirds race up and down the pebbly coast, chasing one another in and out of shallow pools.

I take out my journal and close my eyes, listening to the gentle lapping of the water, the wind rustling the trees. The melody is still there, but every time I try to put words to the notes, it feels wrong. Eventually, the whole thing slips away.

My eyes snap open. There's a frustrated whirring in my chest. This used to be so easy. Ever since I was young,

I've been able to write full songs in the shower. It would start with a silly rhyme, a catchy jingle, and before I'd even realized what was happening, the verses, the bridge, the whole thing would practically write itself. But even then, when I hadn't even had my first relationship, the songs were about boys: wanting them, feeling ignored by them, dreaming of the one I would never let go.

Now when I try to write *new* words, I'm lost. Literally lost, like there was a road I used to take and now I can't seem to find it. Like it's overgrown or paved over, or I'm in the wrong part of town. I look up at the trees, a low, groan stuck in the back of my throat. How did I end up here? And how do I get back?

Without thinking, I take out my phone and my journal. I open to the page with Noel's number and I punch it into the keypad. My thumbs fly across the screen.

Hey.
It's Lily.

I hit Send and hold my breath, before letting the air out in one giant, calming whoosh. I feel surprisingly tired for somebody who has been on vacation for three weeks. I bury my head in my hands, my phone pressed against my forehead. Why do I always do this? Why, when I need inspiration, when I'm feeling stalled or blocked, do I assume that attention from a boy will help? Is my songwriting ability inexorably tied to my inability to stop thinking about boys? The idea makes me feel cringey and weak.

The phone buzzes between my temples and I jump.

Noel: Lily who?

My stomach does a flip-flop as I stare at the screen. *Lily who?*

The phone buzzes again.

Noel: Just kidding.

I laugh and scramble to type back.

Me: You're funny.
Noel: I try. What's up?
Me: Tess dragged me on a hike.
Noel: Which one?
Me: I'm not sure. There's a creek. And blueberries.
Noel: You'll need to be more specific.
Me: There are these cute little islands.
Noel: Pease's Point?
Me: Yes!

Noel: Cool. Look for the floating cabin.

Me: The what?

Noel: Where are you now?

Me: On a bench. I'm supposed to be writing.

Noel: Walk up and around the next bend.
There's a trail marker and a tree that
looks like a monkey.

I look over my shoulder, as if he might be watching me somehow, and stand. His directions lead me up a hill and around the corner, until I spot a white signpost near the ground. Beside it is a small, knotty tree, its limbs contorted into unmistakably monkey-esque shapes.

Me: It really does look like a monkey!

Noel: I know.

Me: Okay. Now what?

Noel: Now turn around.

I turn and look down. There's a small inlet tucked between two clusters of giant evergreens. In the middle of the water, floating all alone, is a tiny cottage with a red shingled roof and a bright yellow door. It sits on a square dock and bobs gently up and down in the current, like it might drift off down the creek and disappear into the ocean.

I smile as I hold up my phone. I snap a quick photo and send it to him.

Me: I love it.

Noel: I thought you might.

Me: Who lives there?

Noel: Nobody anymore. The town takes care of it.

Noel: When I was little there was this old guy who lived out there by himself after his wife died. They used to sail together and when he got too old to take care of the boat, he wanted to live on the water. So he built a floating cabin.

Me: What happened to him?

Noel: He died a year after she did. To the day.

Me: Guess they couldn't stand to be apart.

Noel: Maybe.

Noel: Or maybe there was something in the water.

I laugh, a short, hard cackle, and a trio of birds scatters from the bushes beside me.

"What's so funny?"

I whip around to see Tess standing behind me, her cheeks pink from climbing.

I tuck the phone guiltily into my pocket. "Nothing. Just Terry. He sent some new ideas from wardrobe for the tour."

"That bad?" Tess loves to poke fun at the crazy things my style team comes up with. Last tour, she called me "Bubblegum Barbie" for two months straight.

I swallow. I hate lying, but I tell myself it's for the best. The last thing I need is a speech from Tess about boys. If anyone knows what I'm doing is wrong, it's me. But there's that little part of me that does wonder if I *need* this, if I'm unable to write without it. "Yeah, it's absurd," I say. "I'll show you later."

I start back up the trail. "Come on," I call back to her. "I want to see this famous view." I keep moving, my heart pounding in my chest, my phone buzzing in my pocket, holding my breath until I hear the familiar shuffle of Tess's boots scurrying behind me.

11

"ARE THOSE THE shoes you're wearing?"

It's late, almost ten o'clock, and Noel meets me behind the house at the top of the rickety beach staircase. I'm wearing my favorite lace-up ankle boots, and one heel is caught between the slats of the wooden deck.

"You said it wasn't a long walk," I whisper. We're hidden from the house by a wall of tall shrubs, but I remember how far voices carry in the ocean breeze.

"It's not long," Noel says, grinning. "But it is . . . you know . . . in nature." He points toward a small opening in the trees, the beginning of a path I haven't seen before. "This way."

It was my idea to meet at night. Noel suggested

lunch, or another ride on his boat, but there was the issue of potentially being photographed with a new guy so soon after the breakup. And more important, I didn't want to hear about it from Tess and Sammy. They'd say all the things I already knew: it's too soon, I always do this, I need more time by myself. But while I need to write new music, I'm also here to unwind. To have fun. And spending time with Noel—texting him, thinking about him—is the first time I've felt relaxed since I got here.

"Almost there," Noel encourages from a few paces ahead. His phone lights the trail between us, and he glances back often to make sure I'm all right.

Noel had said he wanted to show me something, but now, tiptoeing over rocks in heels in the dark, I wish I'd at least told Ray where I was going. I can just imagine a new crop of headlines:

Lily Ross Left for Dead by Strange Man in the Woods
Quest for Love Kills Starry-Eyed Singer

I'm about to ask if we should turn back when the trail stops abruptly and the trees open onto a clearing at the edge of a cliff.

"What do you think?" Noel asks, holding an arm out over an enormous, bean-shaped pond. It's ringed by tidy formations of tall, feathery trees, and the moon shimmers on the smooth black water. It's breathtaking, in a surreal sort of way, like we've stumbled into the pages of a picture book.

"Not bad, huh?" Noel asks, leading me down another steep path to a jutting lower ledge.

"What is this place?"

"It's the quarry," Noel says. "My favorite swimming hole on the island." I look quickly down at my high-waisted shirtdress: wardrobe strike two. "We don't have to go in," he assures me. "I just wanted you to see it."

He wipes dirt and pine needles from the surface of a square ledge of granite and gestures for me to sit. "I come out here sometimes to look at the stars," he says, gesturing to the sky, which is totally clear, the constellations lit up like billboards.

"It's beautiful."

Noel disappears behind a cluster of trees, pine needles rustling as he tromps through the underbrush. Eventually he reappears with an armful of knotted sticks. He drops them with a clatter into a sunken spot at the edge of the woods. It's a fire pit, dug into the ground and charred from years of use.

"Need some help?" I ask. I quickly untie the laces of my boots and leave them on the ledge behind me.

"Careful," he says, glancing with concern at my bare feet. "I can do it."

"I know you can," I say, following him with deliberate

steps into the thick brush. I let Noel do the heavy lifting but find some smaller twigs and branches and toss them into the pile. Once we've gathered enough kindling, Noel pulls a book of matches from his pocket and lights one.

Soon, the fire is roaring. We sit together on a fallen log, staring at the flames in silence, lost in the rhythm of popping sparks and crackles. "I could probably do this for hours and be happy," I say, the skin on my legs and my cheeks slowly warming. "It's hypnotic."

"Better than TV," Noel agrees. "We used to go camping every summer. My mom built the best fires. They were more like installation pieces. You almost felt bad watching them fall apart."

"My mom can't even light my birthday candles," I say. "She's not exactly outdoorsy." I feel a sharp pang of homesickness—not for New York but for Madison, where my parents are. I'd give anything to be driving around with Dad, singing along to his favorites: the Beatles, the Rolling Stones. Or wrapped up in one of Mom's killer hugs, smelling her gardenia perfume.

"This place is sort of like a bubble," I say, looking out over the still water. "The island, I mean. It's so easy to forget that the outside world exists."

"I think that's what people like about it," Noel says. "In the seventies it was this haven for famous artists. I guess they liked that nobody knew or cared who they were."

It feels so true, even if I'm not entirely incognito here. I remember the way Noel looked at me the first time we met, standing between our mangled cars: like I could have been anyone. "You knew who I was when I hit you," I tease him. "Even if you did a good job faking it."

Noel fans away a cloud of gray smoke. "I think I was in shock," he says. "And I guess it's in my DNA. It's a real live-and-let-live approach here, especially when it comes to *celebrities*."

I cringe. "I hate that word."

"Why?" Noel asks with a smile. "You're the best of the best. That's worth celebrating."

"I guess so." My eyes blur as I stare into the flames. "Though it doesn't feel like I'm the best at anything, lately."

"Writer's block?" Noel asks.

"How'd you guess?"

"Lots of people come here for inspiration," he says, poking at the fire with a stick. "Don't give up yet."

He tends the fire with quick, confident movements. There's something in the way he holds his head and shoulders, the way he carefully selects his words, that makes it almost impossible not to trust him.

He drops the stick into the fire and leans back,

rubbing his hands together. His fingers are big and calloused, but his nails look like they've been scrubbed clean. Around his wrist is a thick rope bracelet that looks like it was once white but is now gray, the seams loose and fraying.

He catches me staring. "Sidney," he says, twisting the bracelet around his wrist. "My sister. She made them for Christmas a few years back. We all have one."

"Do you have other siblings?" I ask.

"Just me and Sid," he says. "And my dad."

"What about your mom?" I ask without thinking. There's a heavy pause and I feel my pulse quicken. It's the first time I've talked like this to anyone in years. There's a strange, assumed familiarity that happens when you chat with other people in the business. Before Jed even opened his mouth I knew all about his upbringing in California. I knew his parents were famous session musicians and that he had an older brother in rehab. Getting to know someone through conversation, from the very beginning, feels startlingly intimate.

"She's not really around," Noel says quietly before quickly adding: "She's not dead. She left a few years ago. She's a painter. Used to teach at the high school. Everyone loved her. But she always felt like she should be doing more. Seeing more. She traveled a lot before we were born."

I turn to look at him, the orange of the fire jumping in his clear blue eyes. "So she just . . . left?"

Noel shrugs. "Pretty much. It was hard for Sid. My dad is out most nights on the boat. It wasn't good for her to spend so much time alone."

"So that's why you came back. To help out?"

Noel pokes at the fire with a stick. "It didn't make sense to be away." It looks like he wants to say more, and I get the feeling that this is a theme. Like just beneath the surface of every silence is a whole conversation, fighting to be let out.

"Do you ever miss it?" I ask.

Noel tosses the stick into the fire and fidgets with the sleeves of his shirt. "Miss what?"

"School? Life off the island?"

Noel looks down at his feet, shuffling them against a bed of pine needles.

"I'm sorry," I say abruptly. "I ask too many questions."

He twists his rope bracelet lightly against the hard knobs of his wrist, still not looking up. "It's okay."

"I wasn't always like this," I confess. "I had to be trained. If I didn't ask questions, I was going to have to answer them. Backstage. At appearances. So I learned to investigate. Most people like talking about themselves."

Noel smiles shyly. "Guess I'm not most people."

"Quiet is okay, too," I say.

"I'm not always quiet," he responds. "Just when I'm nervous."

I remember him behind the wheel of his boat, or crouching under the smoking debris of his truck. "I wouldn't have pegged you for the nervous type."

"I'm not," he says, flipping his palms over his lap and letting out an exasperated sigh like a little kid, frustrated by a half-finished puzzle. "Not usually."

I put my hand over his, weaving my narrow fingers inside his strong ones. His skin is softer than I thought it would be, and warm from the fire. He looks at me, almost timidly, as if he's asking permission, his eyes searching mine, and before I know it I'm leaning in and kissing him softly on the lips. I don't even think about it—if I did, I'd surely realize it's a mistake—but instinct takes over. Noel doesn't pull back or move closer, just kisses me back gently.

"Sorry," I say, abruptly pulling away. "Was that okay?"

Noel smirks. "You really do ask too many questions." He pushes a stray hair back behind my ear and kisses me again, this time harder, like he means it. Like it's what he's been trying to say all night.

12

76 Days Until Tour
June 28th

SUNDAY, 2:35 A.M.

Me: Are you awake?

Noel: No.

…

Noel: Haha.

Me: I can't sleep.

Noel: Me neither.

…

…

Noel: How's your ankle? That was a nasty fall.

Me: I didn't fall! I was skipping.

Noel: Looked pretty swollen.

Me: That's just the way my ankles look.

Noel: Lily Ross has cankles!

Me: Don't tell.

Noel: It will be our secret.

…

Noel: I had fun.

Me: Me too.

…

…

Noel: I have to go out on the boat tomorrow night.

Me: All night?

Noel: Pretty much. It's my dad's night off.

Me: Can I come?

Noel: It's pretty rugged.

Me: I can handle it.

Noel: Promise not to judge my music?

Me: Promise.

…

Me: Unless you listen to those rappers that dress up like clowns.

Noel: That's a thing?

Me: Good answer.

The next day crawls by, each hour like a lifetime. Tess and Sammy and I sit by the beach and go for long walks.

Sammy picks up fancy salads from the vegan organic takeout place but I can barely eat a bite. All I can do is think about Noel, the way his eyes glowed in the fire, the way his fingers felt wrapped up in mine. I don't think about my music or my tour at all.

Addict.

That night, after Tess falls asleep in front of a documentary about graffiti artists and Sammy goes up to her room, I sneak out the back door again. Noel and I arranged a meeting spot at a dock farther down the beach. When I get there, I see his boat bobbing in the dark. Noel leans against a wooden post beside it, the sleeves of his sweater pushed up to his elbows.

The water is still and quiet and there's a chill in the air. This time I'm dressed for the occasion in a big knit sweater, jeans, and Converse slip-ons, but the wind whips my hair into a wild mess as soon as we're out on the open water. If anything, this trip is teaching me that I can't micromanage my appearance when the elements are involved.

I help Noel haul in the traps for a while, but when I get tired I sit on the bench, watching as he works. His movements are slow and almost graceful, like he's doing his own sort of yoga in the dark. He's so focused that I try not to interrupt him. At first, the quiet is unsettling. It's hard for me sit with my thoughts for so long without having anybody to bounce them back at me. But I force myself to listen, to feel the spray of salt on my hands and forehead, to watch the horizon for signs of morning.

After about an hour, I give up.

"Can I ask you something?"

Noel smirks as he steers the boat around a passage of half-sunken rocks. "Not talking is killing you, isn't it?"

"What do you mean? I'm so Zen I've practically reached enlightenment. Soon I'll be nothing more than a glowing ball of light."

Noel kills the motor as we pull up alongside yet another buoy. "Go ahead," he says. "But I have to warn you, my life is about as interesting as that pile of rocks back there."

"I love rocks."

Noel chuckles. "Ask away."

I watch the muscles on the back of his arms tense and release as he struggles with the rope in the water. "Do you ever think about leaving again?" I ask.

Noel reaches up and attaches the rope to a pulley overhead. "Sometimes," he says, tugging down on the rope to test it. "I liked school. I think about going back."

"Where were you?" I ask.

"Boston," he says. "Mass Art. I wanted to get into graphic design."

I try to imagine him on a computer or doing anything that requires working indoors. "You're kidding," I say. "Art school?"

"Yeah." He shrugs and sits down beside me. "Why? I don't strike you as the artsy type?"

"No, not that," I say, hoping I haven't offended him. "I just had no idea."

"I've always liked to draw," he says self-consciously.

"Like your mom," I say, and quickly wish that I hadn't. His posture shifts, he sits taller, his shoulders close off like he's hiding something he doesn't want me to see.

"No," he says softly. "Not really. She was—she's a painter. I was just messing around. Stupid stuff. Anyway, I don't do it anymore."

"Why not?"

He scratches the side of his jaw roughly, squinting up at the moon. "Haven't really felt like it," he says. "I don't have a lot of free time. And when I do, there are things I'd rather be doing."

He smiles at me as he says this, and I feel him opening back up. I nuzzle beside him, my head resting in the gentle crook of his shoulder.

"Oh yeah?" I tease. "Like what?"

"Oh, I don't know," he says, shifting on the bench so the sides of our legs are touching. "Lots of things."

He wraps one arm behind my neck and we sit back

against the boat, gazing out across the water. The sky is streaked with orange and pink along the horizon, the sun pushing up against a low layer of heavy clouds.

"Like this?" I ask, my chin jutting out toward the magnificent predawn sky. I reach up and lace my fingers into his, pulling his arm tighter around my shoulder.

"Like this." He smiles and we wait for the show to begin.

Noel drops me at the dock before motoring toward the harbor to unload. I know I should go home and sleep. Sammy and Tess will be up soon, and there's no way they'll let me hide in my room all day without asking questions. But my skin is buzzing and my mind is clear in a way it hasn't been in ages.

Instead of walking back to the house, I head toward the quarry. The sky is still in that sleepy place between dark and daylight, and the birds are just starting to stir. I notice things happening around me that I've never thought to notice before. Usually my brain is on overdrive, struggling to keep up with schedules, sessions, planning for whatever is on deck. Next week, next month, next year; the future is as much a part of my everyday existence as the present. But here I feel like I'm exactly where I should be, like everything that matters is happening right now.

I sit at the edge of the quarry and shiver in the early morning cold, wishing Noel were here to keep me warm, to build me a fire. I smile, remembering the way his arm felt, solid and strong behind my shoulder. But it's more than that. Being around him is so easy because I don't have to be Lily Ross the business. I can just be myself. I haven't had that in any of my other relationships ever, not even with Sebastian, who I met when I was first starting out. Noel is different from the others—he probably doesn't know how to style himself for a red carpet event—but it's a kind of different that makes me feel more like myself than I have in a long, long time.

There's a quiet shushing, the trees bending in a gust of wind, and I close my eyes. This place feels essential; it's everything you need, no more and no less. It's peaceful mornings, strong coffee, and a good book. It's work that gets your hands dirty and an outdoor shower under the stars. It's stars, by the thousands, freed from the competition of man-made glow. I could get used to living here, I think.

My eyes snap open, and before I even have to chase it, the melody is back, the one I lost the other morning. I begin to hum and feel an echo vibrating in the air all around me, like a chorus.

Suddenly, the words are there, too. It's the song I

started on the beach, about waking up and not remembering where you are and why. Only now, there's something almost sweet about forgetting. There's something in starting a new day, with no attachments, nothing pulling you back into the past or rushing you into the future. A yellow-white glow bursts through the trees and I think about the rising sun: strong, hopeful, ready for anything.

The lyrics pour out all at once, just the way they used to when I was a kid, singing into the blue-and-white tiles of my parents' bathroom walls.

The sun is up, a brand-new day
A different world when I'm away.
A tiny house out in the sea
A floating peace, a piece of me.

The sun forgets, there is no past
Today, tomorrow, built to last.
A boat that never leaves the shore
The anchor I've been searching for.

Traps are tangled, set below.
Build a fire, watch it glow.
The things I'll know, the words we'll say.
Anchor's down, I'm here to stay.

13

70 Days Until Tour
July 4th

"YOUR GUITAR WILL still be there when we get back."

Tess pulls the Pree up to a rambling Victorian home at the end of Main Street as Sammy reaches into the backseat for the picnic basket. "Come on," she urges. "You love parades."

I follow them out of the car and up onto the wide front porch of Latham's grandparents' house. The railings are draped in patriotic bunting and a giant flag hangs over the doorway. Sammy's right: I do love parades, and it's been a while since I've been able to watch one as a nameless face in the crowd. But when Tess announced that Latham had invited us to watch the island's Fourth of July celebration from the privacy of his family's balcony, I was anxious more than anything else.

I still haven't told either Tess or Sammy that I've been spending time with Noel. I hate sneaking around, but I'm not ready. Things with Noel are so easy, a stress-free escape. And exploring the island with him has been just the creative spark that I've needed. I don't want to risk losing that by making it public, even—or maybe especially—among my closest friends.

It's been a week since that night at the quarry, and the songs have been pouring out. The first one, "Anchors," led to the next, "At Sea," a narrative ballad about the floating cabin couple. I imagined their love story, from start to finish—their small-town courtship and Saturday-morning routines.

Then came one about a group of boys and girls I watched fishing off the jetty behind our house. They were young, maybe ten or eleven, and I watched them for over an hour. I closed my eyes and listened to the cadence of their voices as they hunted for treasures in the rocks. Their lives—without the complications of romantic love—seemed so carefree. I turned the scene into a song called "Skipping Stones" by lunchtime.

And just last night, after Sammy and Tess went to bed, I looked through one of Tess's family photo albums and jotted down notes for a song called "Summer Stay." It's a somewhat fictionalized account of a beloved vacation home that sees a young girl through her parents' divorce. It's the first time I've ever written about one of my friends directly, and I feel a nervous flutter in my chest when I think about sharing it with Tess.

As Tess rings the bell I notice Noel's truck wedged up on the lawn. A swirl of butterflies zips around my stomach. We have a plan to play things cool, but even so: I can't wait to see him.

J.T. swings the grand front door inward and gestures gallantly to the foyer. "Ladies." His scruffy beard has been tamed and he wears khaki shorts and a stiff red polo that looks newly bought. I imagine it's the first time he's gotten "dressed up" all year and I'm surprisingly touched by the effort. I peer behind J.T. at the sitting room, formally appointed with upholstered chairs and a crystal chandelier.

"Are you sure we're allowed to be in here?" Tess asks as we follow him up the carpeted main staircase to the second floor. French doors off the landing lead to a long, narrow balcony. Latham waits outside wearing a red-white-and-blue–striped button-down. He offers us noisemakers as we join him.

"Are you kidding?" Latham asks. "My grandmother just about collapsed when I told her you were coming. Although she did ask for a picture. She wants to show it off at church."

I smile. "I'd be honored. Where is she now?"

"They live in Florida," Latham explains, pouring us each a plastic cup of iced tea from a pitcher on the balcony table. "They used to spend summers here, but now it's getting harder to travel."

There's a brush of air behind me and I turn to see Noel opening the door. Of the three of them, he's dressed the most casually, in a plain white T-shirt and olive-green shorts. As he passes, I can smell the familiar hints of his shampoo, and my heart races. My eyes land on the crook of his tanned neck and shoulder, where just last night my head was resting. I flash him a quick smile and he gives me a conspiratorial nod, before greeting Tess with a warm hug.

"I didn't know you were going to be here." Tess smiles, shoving him playfully in the side. "You used to hate this parade. You said it was for tourists and two-year-olds."

Noel's cheeks redden and he shrugs. "I guess it's growing on me," he says. "Especially now that we don't have to watch it with the riffraff."

He gestures to the street where the crowds are starting to gather, lining the curb three-deep. Kids in strollers lick messy ice cream cones while their parents navigate potholes in the pavement, searching for the perfect parade-watching spot. Police officers stand on patrol, cutting off traffic with simple barricades. In the distance, I start to hear the patter of marching band drums, the trill of trumpets and horns.

We move to the far side of the wraparound balcony, craning to see the approaching procession. The first rows of synchronized players march into view, flanked by bright banners and teenage girls with batons. Behind them, a cluster of elderly veterans smile at the crowd, some pushing others in wheelchairs, waving to friends and neighbors on the sidelines and tossing candy to the crowd.

I feel my eyes getting damp. Grandpa and his army buddies always march in our parade back home, and I used to help him get ready, hoping he'd sneak me a piece of candy before lining up in formation. Fourth of July has always been my favorite holiday, although in recent years I've moved on to more elaborate traditions. Last year I convinced Jed to throw an epic party at his house in the Hamptons, complete with water slides and private fireworks over the water. It was two hundred people I barely knew, but I loved every minute of it. It's strange that I can be equally satisfied, dressed to the nines and hosting a catered affair, or gleefully blowing into a plastic party favor as I cheer on a town parade.

The guys—who have been busy reminiscing about the years they marched as Boy Scouts or captains of various sports teams—join us on our side of the balcony. As Noel passes, he finds my hand for a clandestine squeeze, and I feel a thrilling jolt. He whistles to a pair of old ladies, inching past in a vintage car. They honk and wave, and I find myself enthusiastically waving back, as if I'm front row at somebody else's concert, giddy to be part of the crowd.

Night falls. Birds quiet, cicadas hum, the sapphire sky turns purple, then black. I sit alone on the screened porch with my journal, working out new lyrics. I had the idea on the way home from the parade. The song is called "July," and it's about the joys of unwrapping candy, sparklers and fireworks and the ways the holiday changes as a girl grows older. It's about innocence, and finding what's been lost. I'm half-singing the melody when Tess knocks on the door, her dark hair wavy and wet from the shower.

"You're sure you don't want to come?" she asks, folding a thin quilt and stuffing it into a bag over her shoulder. Sammy appears behind her, adorable in a white skirt and red-and-white-striped halter. Her freckled skin has turned a light bronze, her strawberry hair lightening to blond at the tips.

The guys told us about a spot on the point where

everyone goes to watch the fireworks. I'd thought it would be the perfect place for Noel and me to sneak away—we could duck behind the lit-up dunes and share a secret kiss to the soundtrack of the booming lights and *ooh*s and *aah*s of the crowd on the beach. But after we left, Noel texted that he had other ideas.

I check the time quickly on my phone, then nod at my guitar on the cushioned bench beside me. "We've got work to do," I say. "But you guys go ahead. I'll be fine."

Sammy gives me a thumbs-up and follows Tess outside. Once their headlights have disappeared, I pack up my guitar and fold my journal shut. My heart feels heavy. As much as I'm trying to avoid it, there's a distance growing between my friends and me, and it makes me feel unsteady, like I'm walking a tightrope, constantly lunging from one side to the other, desperate to stay upright.

But as I speed-walk down the moonlit trail, squinting toward the rickety dock where Noel and his boat are waiting, the guilt and discomfort fade away, an eager, bubbling anticipation filling me up in their place.

Noel waves, and I start to skip toward him, holding my hands out like I'm flying. When I reach him I wrap my arms around his sturdy waist. "Sorry I'm late," I say, slightly out of breath.

"Skipping's hard work," he teases, ruffling the top of my hair.

He helps me onto the boat and we motor away from the shore. There's a cluster of boats gathered around the harbor, mainlanders coming to anchor for the show. Noel steers around them toward a secluded spot farther away. When there's not another boat or building in sight, he cuts the engine, and we bob in the quiet on the calm waters.

"My dad used to take us out here," he says, twisting the top of a thermos and handing it to me. I take a sip: warm cider, with hints of orange and cinnamon, perfect for the chilly night. "I used to hate it. All my friends would be at the beach or in the harbor. But he said fireworks were made to be seen from a distance."

Noel takes a sip of cider and wedges the thermos into a cup holder. "And now you agree?" I ask.

Noel shrugs. "We'll find out," he says. "I haven't watched the fireworks in years."

I scoff playfully. "No parades, no fireworks?" I ask. "What kind of all-American boy are you?"

Noel half smiles, his lower lip caught between his teeth. "Not a very good one, I guess. I don't know. I was away, and now I'm usually busy working. I don't get a lot of time off."

Unease roils my stomach. Of course he's been busy. He's basically supporting his family, raising his little sister. Not everyone has the luxury of planning parties at every occasion.

"But mostly I just haven't had anyone to watch them with," he says, giving my waist a nudge with his elbow.

"I find that hard to believe," I say. "I have a feeling the Noel Bradley fan club is not lacking for members."

Noel rubs a calloused hand over his lightly stubbled chin. "It used to be bigger," he concedes.

"I'm not afraid of a little competition," I say, tilting my face to plant a kiss on the side of his strong jaw. "As long as I can be board president."

He turns to kiss me on the lips, then pulls away. His eyes are full of something, like he's searching for words again. I quickly kiss his nose.

"Let's go in," I say, glancing out over his shoulder at the shimmering black water.

"In?" he repeats with a bemused chuckle. But I'm already undressing, peeling off my outer layers and feeling the prickle of cool night air on my skin. I stand in my bra and underwear on the lip of the boat's edge. Noel looks at me disbelievingly and I give him a smile before arching my hands over my head and diving.

The water is freezing, a numbing, arctic shock, but when I resurface the air feels warmer, and my body tingles, like my limbs are suddenly electric. "It's amazing!" I shout back to the boat, but Noel is already airborne, diving over my head. He slips into the water behind me, and as he comes up for air, his legs tangle with mine.

"You're out of your mind." He shivers, hugging me tight.

I laugh into the cold, wet brush of his hair. "Probably."

"Thank you," he says, whispering into my ear.

"For what?"

"For this." He splashes the water between us. "For skipping."

I pull back to look at him, his teeth lightly chattering, his big blue eyes searching mine. In the distance there's a high-pitched squeal and a trail of light shoots up from the water. The first pop echoes around the island, a shimmery white explosion bursting overhead. We tread water and stare with our mouths hanging open, mid-smile, ready for our own private show.

14

67 Days Until Tour
July 7th

"TELL ME SOMETHING good."

Terry's voice is clipped, like he's trying not to panic. It's early in the morning and I wonder how many cups of coffee he's had, and if he's been sleeping on the leather couch in his office, as he typically does when he's worked up.

"Well, I've written five songs and I think I have our first single," I say nonchalantly, leaning back into the lawn chair on the back porch. "Does that count as good?" Tess and Sammy are still sleeping—they were out late at a beach bonfire last night—and I'm trying to keep my voice low, but Terry's exuberant screeches and hollers are probably loud enough to wake them.

"I knew it!" he shouts. "I *knew* you could do it." I don't bother to remind him that he hadn't sounded wholly convinced the last time we spoke. "When can I hear them?"

I laugh and stretch my tanned legs out toward the deck railing. "I've done a few rough cuts on my phone. I can send them now."

Terry whoops again and I can practically hear him composing emails to the label guys and publicity team, rushing to plan sessions. "Great, great," he murmurs distractedly. "And when are you coming back?"

My smile tightens and I clear my throat. "That's the thing," I say carefully. "I'm not."

I hear the clacking of Terry's fingers on the keys pause and pick up again, the slight hiccup in his breathing. "What do you mean?"

"I want to stay until the end of the summer," I say. "Things are going so well, I'm writing like crazy, and I think it would be . . . irresponsible to come back to the city now."

I hold my breath and wait. It's all true; I have been feeling more creatively inspired than ever before. Though occasionally, thoughts of Jed still creep in, I've managed to find a way to stay focused, and the new songs have been coming from an entirely different place. It's a place that's linked to my life and environment, my friends, but most of all, the island, and not a breakup or particular person.

But as I'm talking I hear the uneven pitch of my voice and I know I'm not being totally honest. There's another reason I don't want to leave so soon. A five-foot-ten-inch, charmingly aloof, and ruggedly handsome reason named Noel. And even if the songs aren't about him, I'm a little panicked that this new well of creativity would dry up if our relationship suddenly ended.

"I was thinking we could record out here," I eagerly continue.

"Out there?" Terry chuckles. "Where, on the beach?"

"Why not?" I ask. "This place . . . just wait until you see it, Terry. It's really special. And I've been feeling . . . I'm ready to do something different. I've given it a lot of thought."

Terry sighs, the familiar sigh of surrender. He can tell that I've made up my mind.

"You're the boss," he says at last. "I'll handle everything."

"Thanks, Terry." I smile. "I owe you."

"What else is new," he mutters, but I know he's smiling, too.

We hang up and I scroll around my phone, looking for the most recent recording I've made of "Anchors." It's the perfect song for a single, up-tempo enough but unlike anything I've done before. I send it to Terry in an email and rush inside, already feeling better.

Tess and Sam are in the kitchen when I get there, brewing coffee and ladling spoonfuls of yogurt into ceramic bowls.

"Morning, sunshines!" I reach into the fridge to pour myself a glass of the fresh-squeezed orange juice Tess brought back from the farmers' market last Sunday.

"What's her problem?" Tess grumbles to Sammy, her eyes puffy and still not totally open.

"I have the opposite of problems," I say cheerily. "I have great news."

"You found a place with real coffee on this island?" Tess asks, wincing as she pours the last of the bag she brought with her into the paper filter.

"I just talked to Terry," I say. "And we're going to record here!"

Sammy looks around the kitchen. "Where?" she asks as if I might set up a sound booth in the pantry.

"On the island," I say. "That way I don't have to leave. The guys will bring everything we need. They'll only stay for a few days . . ."

"Stay here?" Tess asks. "In this house?"

I turn quickly to look at her. "Sure," I say. "That's all right, isn't it?"

A series of expressions I can't quite read flashes across her face.

"Or at the B and B in town," I backtrack. "Whatever you want. I just thought you'd be happy we don't have to race back to the city."

Sammy nods encouragingly at Tess. "We are happy."

I see Tess's shoulders drop almost imperceptibly. "Of course we're happy," she says finally. "It will be fun."

"Great," I say, staring over their heads into the screened-in porch. "I was thinking we could record out there. It will take some work getting things ready . . ."

"We're on it," Sammy says, scarfing down the last of her yogurt. Tess's phone buzzes on the table and she picks it up. I can tell by the low cinch of her brow that it's Terry. The wheels are in motion, the work is about to begin.

Terry arrives on the first boat Thursday morning. Ray and K2 take me to the harbor to meet him and I feel the way I did on visiting day at camp, scanning the line of slow-moving cars for my parents' navy-blue Honda Civic: one part giddy about seeing a familiar face and one part anxious, not sure I'm ready for two worlds to collide.

The boat pulls slowly into the slip. Terry is standing behind the chain on the lower deck, wearing dark jeans and a white linen shirt, a leather messenger bag slung over one shoulder. Even from across the parking lot I can see that his hair, usually gelled into sleek points, is slightly overgrown, and there are dark, tired shadows under his eyes.

"You couldn't have hidden out in the Hamptons?" Terry barks as he walks briskly to the car. I squeeze him in a hug. I've spent so much of my time here trying to avoid him and his questions that I haven't realized how much I've missed him. Terry complains more than anyone I know, but he has believed in me from the very beginning. From our first meeting at an open mic in Madison, to the early, brutal days of all-night signings and meet-and-greets in every state, he's seen me through every career move, every up and down. Next to my parents, I trust him more than anyone on the planet, and as strange as it is to be suddenly thrust back into work mode, it feels right that he's here.

Terry shakes hands with Ray and K2 and we climb into the backseat. I hand him the coffee we picked up on the way. I feel a little bit like a matchmaker, sitting in on a first date between Terry and the island. I roll down the window and take a deep breath, trying to see the quaint town, the meandering coast, through new eyes.

"You're really going to love it here," I say, beaming as the car bumps around a pothole.

"Lil, I don't care if you had to live in a van under the Brooklyn Bridge," he says, wiping a drop of spilled coffee from the knee of his jeans. "If it makes you write songs like these new ones, it's paradise."

"Really?" It's always nerve-racking getting feedback, especially from Terry. When new material starts to come out, it feels so mysterious. If I don't get it right the first time, I always fear that I won't be able to get back to that inspired place ever again.

Terry nods matter-of-factly. "Really." He rubs his hands over his eyes and sighs. "I gotta say, you gave us all a real scare. I thought you were pulling some Britney Spears shit."

I give Terry's shoulder a shove as we pull out of town and start up the long dirt road to the house. "No, you didn't."

Terry squeezes my fingers. "No," he says. "I didn't. But I didn't know you had *this* in you, either."

I smile. "That good?"

I always get chills when I hear somebody talk about my music in a way that makes it seem like it's not just mine. I put so much of myself into my songs, sometimes I forget that anybody else will ever hear them.

"Here we are," I say as K2 slows to a stop, dust kicking up around us.

Terry leans across me to get a better look. "This is

where you've been staying?" he asks incredulously as I climb out first.

I bound excitedly up the uneven front steps. "Isn't it fantastic?"

"It's something . . ." Terry grumbles, following me inside. Sam is in the kitchen making waffles and Tess is sprawled on the couch with her phone. They both jump when they see us, running into the crowded hall.

"Terry!" Sam squeals, wrapping her arms around his neck.

Tess unravels Terry's bag from his shoulder. "Tell me you brought provisions."

Terry walks pointedly into the small kitchen and stands over the sink, dramatically emptying out the sludgy contents of the cup I brought him down the drain. "Never fear, ladies," he says, reaching into his bag and pulling out a paper bag of the trendy imported coffee beans he has delivered to his office every week. "Terry's here."

15

65 Days Until Tour
July 9th

AS SOON AS the guys from the label—a producer and an engineer—arrive later that afternoon, the world starts to move in double-time. Laptops are opened, levels are adjusted, microphones set up in makeshift booths. I feel a new energy coursing through me, that satisfying thrill of everything clicking into place.

The producer, Nigel, is new to the label and I haven't worked with him before. He's from London, and we chat for a while about which venues I've played and where to get the best fish-and-chips. I like him right away; he's brimming with ideas for the track. Even though I've done this a billion times, it still feels thrilling that everyone in the room is excited about something I've written.

The next morning, we set up on the screened-in side porch. Nigel wants to get some authentic ambient sounds, like seagulls and waves. He asks me to play the song exactly the way it came out. Tess runs to my room to grab my guitar, while Sammy makes sure the porch is stocked with snacks and water. She puts a kettle on for my favorite ginger tea and opens a new box of honey sticks. I suck on one to coat my throat and flip to the lyrics in my journal.

Four hours and more than thirty takes later, we break for lunch. It's incredible how quickly time flies when I'm recording. There's so much that goes into laying down a track, so much more than just me singing a song into a microphone. There are decisions to be made about everything from instrumentation to backing vocals to the overall "tone" of the sound. I always start with a general idea about what I want. For "Anchors," I know I want something bold and confident. It's a ballad, but it's not a weepy love song. It's about knowing what I want and how to get it. Nigel seems to understand implicitly.

I look up through the window to see Sammy in the kitchen, rushing to get the table set. She's spent all morning roasting farmers' market veggies and a whole organic chicken from a farm down the road. I watch as she carefully plates the food, trying hard to make everything look presentable. I tap on the glass and wave but she doesn't even glance up.

"You good?" Tess asks as the guys stand up to stretch. The engineer goes out for a cigarette while Terry and Nigel return calls and check email on the porch.

"I'm great." I beam. "How does it sound?"

"Killer." Tess nods overenthusiastically. "Really great."

I eye her skeptically. "Be honest."

She smirks. "Honestly? I haven't heard a single take. I've been helping Sammy coordinate dietary restrictions, and I just got back from an island-wide hunt for sparkling water." She leans in to whisper in a fake accent: "I found club soda but Nigel *much prefers Pellegrino*."

I laugh. Tess does, too, but stops herself. I follow her gaze to the coffee table where a framed photograph of her dad and her brother, on a hammock in the backyard, has been knocked over. Tess bends down to scoop up the frame, dusting off the glass and carrying it out of the room. "Lunch is ready," she calls over her shoulder. "Don't forget to hydrate."

I stand and stretch my arms to the sky. I've been sitting in the same position all morning and my shoulders are in knots. I'm doing a series of stretches that I remember from Maya's yoga class when Terry sneaks back in.

"So when do we get to meet this *anchor*?" he asks,

plopping into the old, tattered armchair beside the big picture window.

"What do you mean?" I sit down with my back to him, reaching to touch my toes. It feels good, but I'm mostly just trying to hide the red splotches that are blooming on my neck and face.

"The lyrics," Terry prods. *"The anchor you've been searching for . . ."*

"Oh." I laugh, a little too loud. "It's just the island. I told you, I'm really falling for this place."

I lie on my back with my knees bent, my bare toes wiggling against the smooth wooden floorboards. Terry stands over me with his arms crossed.

"What?" I ask, maybe a bit too harshly. "Not every song I write has to be about me." The truth is, I'm embarrassed. I wanted to write a fully boy-free album, and though none of the new songs are explicitly love songs . . . it doesn't take much to realize that Noel is in the subtext, bursting from between the lines of every single one.

"Give me a break," Terry says, rolling his eyes. "You couldn't write an inauthentic lyric if your life depended on it."

He nudges my waist with the top of one shiny leather loafer. "The island may be your anchor, but somebody's got you hooked." He smiles back at me on his way into the kitchen. "Whether you're ready to admit it or not."

★ ★ ★

The first two nights of recording we stay up late working and hanging out with Terry. It feels like old times—there's talk about the tour and what comes after, new merch and a holiday album—but by the third day, I'm missing Noel. Before the guys arrived I warned him that things would get crazy, but I've hardly been able to do more than send a good night text.

Saturday morning, I wake up before everyone else and tiptoe down the driveway. K2 is alone in the car and I ask him to drive me to the harbor. Noel was out on the boat all night and he should be just pulling in.

By the time I get to the docks, he's already unloading, his back to me as he slides the crowded crates onto the trembling dock. "Surprise!" I announce, and he starts. "Sorry," I say. "I wanted to be here when you got in."

He stands and wipes a hand along his sweaty brow. It's early but the sun is already beating down. His eyes are tired and red at the corners, but they sparkle to life when he sees me. "There she is," he says, leaning in to give me a salty kiss. "I probably smell like fish guts."

"My favorite." I leap into the boat and feel it sink beneath my weight. "Can I help?"

Noel points to a trap at the far end of the boat. "Push that over," he says, and I do. "How's it going?"

"It's great," I say. "A lot of work, but I think it's going to be worth it. The guys are loving it here. You should've seen them in the ocean."

Between sessions yesterday, we brought Terry and the guys to a small beach on the far side of the island, thinking it would be deserted. By the time we left there were crowds lined up, and I ended up signing everything from Frisbees to swim trunks and even a golden retriever's collar.

"Sounds like I'm the only one who didn't," Noel jokes. He smiles but there's something new and uncertain in his voice.

"Hey." I touch his sun-warmed shoulder. "I know it's a little nuts with them here."

"A little?" Noel drops the last of the traps to the dock with a thud. "The island hasn't had this much to talk about since the Kennedys came for a day-trip in the sixties." He shakes his head. "Your producers aren't exactly *low profile*."

"I know," I say understandingly. "But they'll be gone soon."

Noel nods, clearly unconvinced.

I wrap my arms around his neck and pull him in for a quick kiss. "Nothing changes," I say. "It's just work. I promise."

Over Noel's shoulder, I see a pair of middle-aged women standing on the sidewalk, camera phones poised in midair.

"Crap," I whisper under my breath, letting my arms fall to my sides.

Noel whips around to investigate, a dark cloud settling over his features. "I told you," he says, disheartened.

I stuff my hands into the pockets of my jean shorts. "It will pass," I say. "Once everyone leaves I'll just be a regular girl again."

"You could never be regular," he says with a halfhearted smile. I find his hand for a quick squeeze and promise to call him when everyone leaves, and then I hurry back to the car where K2 is waiting. As I shut myself inside the air-conditioned quiet, I hear Noel's words ringing in my ears. *You could never be regular.* It sounded like a compliment when he'd said it. But now, I'm not so sure.

16

59 Days Until Tour
July 15th

"GOING SOMEWHERE?"

I freeze with one hand on back door, the floorboards creaking beneath me. Sammy is at the bottom of the stairs in her pajamas, a cute striped set that I got for all three of us last Christmas. Her hair is pulled into a messy topknot and she's wearing her glasses. It's late, past midnight, and she announced that she was going to bed hours ago.

"I thought you were asleep," I say.

Sammy eyes me as she opens the refrigerator door, pulling out a pitcher of lemonade. "I got thirsty. What about you? Walking again?"

Since Terry and the guys left three days ago, promising

to be back as soon as I had more songs to record, I've been sneaking out to meet Noel every night. On the few occasions that Tess or Sammy has noticed, I've told them I'm going out walking, searching for more inspiration.

Which isn't *entirely* untrue.

"Yeah." I nod, pulling my long, knit cardigan close. "Terry's really on me to finish this album." He said we could release the first five songs as a special tour tie-in EP, but I'd prefer a whole new album entirely. If I can keep up this pace, it shouldn't be a problem. As long as I don't get distracted.

I steal a glance through the back window. Noel is already on the beach. He's promised to build a fire and we have plans to camp out. Beneath my jeans I'm wearing two layers of thermal tights, and Noel's bringing blankets. I know I should be writing, and I've been fiddling around with new melodies all day, but the idea of spending a whole night with him, talking for hours and waking up to the sun rising over the ocean . . . it sounds too dreamy to pass up. After all, I leave in three and half weeks, and we haven't talked about the future yet. His. Mine. *Ours.*

"Can't wait to hear what you're working on." Sammy smiles, and there's something so totally trusting in her eyes that it makes my heart sore. "What's it called?"

I turn to see Tess shuffling in from the living room, her dark hair a flattened nest from sleeping on the couch.

"What's what called?"

"Sorry," Sammy says. "Did we wake you?"

Tess mumbles and walks zombie-like to the refrigerator door, which she opens and closes without touching anything inside.

"Bird's going for a walk," Sam says. "I was asking about what she's writing."

Tess nods and gives me a sleepy thumbs-up as she stalks toward the stairs. I move back toward the door, but something won't let me go. Every time I leave without telling them where I'm going, it's like a chasm widens between us. I haven't been able to stop thinking about what Terry said. I don't want to be inauthentic. Not in my songs, and not with my friends.

"Guys," I say quietly, my back still to them. "I have to tell you something."

I hear Tess's footsteps pause on the stairs.

"What is it?" Sammy asks. She switches immediately into caretaker mode, pulling out a chair at the table and pushing me down into it. "Is everything okay?"

Tess appears again in the doorway, leaning against the wall, her eyes half shut. "Any chance it can wait until the morning?"

"No, actually." I sigh. "It can't."

I put my hands on the table and flatten my fingertips against the checkered tablecloth. Misshapen splatters of an old coffee stain trail between my thumbs. I take a deep breath.

"I've been seeing someone," I say fast, like ripping off a Band-Aid. I look up into Sammy's eyes, watching the confusion spread across her face. "I wanted to tell you right away, but I made such a big deal about being alone, and I knew you guys would think it was a mistake—"

"Wait," Tess interrupts, suddenly alert. "What do you mean, seeing someone? Tell me it isn't Jed."

"It isn't Jed," I assure her. It's been weeks since he texted and I've managed to break the habit of wondering what he's doing every day, if or when he'll reach out again. But hearing his name still makes my heart cramp.

"Someone in New York?" Sammy guesses.

I shake my head. "Somebody here."

Tess laughs. "Somebody *here*? You don't know anybody here. And you hardly leave the house, unless you're out walking."

I look guiltily back at my hands. Tess pulls out the chair beside me and sits down heavily.

"You're not out walking, are you?"

I shake my head again.

"I knew it! I knew you were being weird. Didn't I say she was being weird?" Tess looks to Sammy.

"Who is it?" Sammy presses. I can hear in her voice that even though she's hurt that I've lied, there's a part of her that's still excited to hear every last detail. Sammy and I have been trading secrets and dishing about our crushes—at first, mostly hers—since we were twelve years old. We practically have our own language.

It's not Sammy I'm worried about.

"It's Noel," I say, my voice a careful whisper.

"Noel?" Tess asks, her eyebrows shooting up. "My Noel?"

I nod, my features tight in a pained wince. "I'm sorry," I say, looking up to meet her eyes. Her face is frozen somewhere between laughter and disbelief. "I should have told you when it started."

"Which was when?" Tess is already cold and distant, her eyes locked on the floor.

"I don't know." I shrug. "Right after we went out on the boat?"

"That was three weeks ago," Sammy says. "You've been lying to us for three weeks?" Any trace of excitement in her eyes has vanished.

The last time I lied to Sammy was probably when we were in the ninth grade. She wanted to sneak out to the movies and I told her I didn't feel well, when really I was scared of getting caught. Instead, I stayed home and binge-watched *Gilmore Girls* reruns with Mom, which was pretty much my idea of a perfect Friday night.

"I'm sorry," I whisper. "I really am."

"Don't apologize to us," Tess says abruptly. "*You're* the one who wanted a change. *You're* the one who said you were tired of all the rebounds, of getting hurt and writing about it." She stands up, her chair screeching against the linoleum. "If you want to keep losing yourself and falling for the wrong people, that's on you."

"Losing myself?" I ask. "I thought you liked Noel."

"This isn't about Noel!" Tess shouts, turning quickly on her heel. I can't remember the last time she raised her voice at me. In fact, I'm not sure it's ever happened. "This is about you. We are your best friends. We are the only people who don't kiss your ass and tell you what you want to hear all the time. Right?"

"Sure," I stammer. "But . . ."

"But what? But only when you ask for it?" Tess stalks back toward me, her hands on her hips. "That's not how real friendships work, Bird. Real friends tell the truth whether it's comfortable or not, and the truth is you're not ready."

I swallow a lump in my throat and look to Sammy for support. She reaches across the table and squeezes my forearm. "She's right," she says. "You're not. You said you wanted things to be different. Bouncing from Jed to somebody else, before you've had time to figure out what you want, for *you* . . . that's exactly what you always do."

I hug my arms around my waist, my heart pounding

in my chest. This is what I was afraid of. Neither of them has any idea what the last few weeks have been like for me, or how Noel, how this whole island, makes me feel. I'm finally able to take a step back and see clearly again. Being with Noel has helped me, not only personally, but creatively. My life is different. My music is different. But I know protesting will only make things worse.

Tess throws up her hands and laughs, a hard cackle. "Now what?" she asks. "Now you write all your songs about Noel? About how he's everything you've ever hoped for, and more? You drag your producers out here every other week to record your *new sound*? To trample all over this house like it's their own private penthouse?"

She shakes her head and swats at the air between us, like she's trying to erase me from her presence. She turns and walks down the hallway, pausing at the stairs. "I should've known bringing you here was a mistake," she says, before loudly climbing up to her room.

Hot tears sting my eyes. Sammy gives my hand another squeeze. I know there are things she wants to say but she doesn't. She doesn't have to. I can read the disappointment all over her face.

"We just care about you," she says evenly. "We don't want to see you get hurt again."

I nod and slip my fingers out of her grasp. My

cheeks are still hot, Tess's words still looping on repeat in my ears.

"You know how she is," Sammy says with a quick glance at the ceiling. "She'll get over it."

"I hope so," I say softly.

"It's just a lot for her."

"What do you mean?"

"Us being here," Sammy says. "This was her place. And now it's . . ."

"Now it's all about me," I say. I remember the morning on the porch with Terry and the guys, the way the whole house was transformed in a matter of minutes. Tess hadn't said a word, but I saw the look in her eyes, the photo on the table, carelessly knocked to its side.

"She'll be fine," Sammy assures me again. "She just needs to blow off some steam."

I nod, wanting to believe her, but knowing that it won't be that easy. Not this time.

Sammy leans back in her chair and yawns.

"Go to sleep," I say. "You look exhausted."

"Want me to stay?" Sammy asks. "I could make you some tea."

I shake my head, biting the insides of my cheeks to keep from crying. I have the best friends in the universe, and all I do is run them ragged. They rally around me and do everything in their power to make sure I have whatever I want, whenever I want it. And this is how I repay them? By lying to them? By doing the one thing I swore I wouldn't do?

"No," I say. "I think I'll just sit for a while."

Sammy nods and gives my shoulder a squeeze. She switches off the light in the hall and turns off the ones in the kitchen, too. I think about asking her to leave them on but don't. I sit in the dark, listening to the hum of the refrigerator and the steady *tick-tick* of the clock on the wall.

Outside, the moon is hidden behind a cloud. I try not to imagine Noel crouching beside the orange glow of a fire as I pull out my phone. It rings five times before going to voice mail. I hang up and text instead.

Can't make it, I type. *Something came up.*

I consider explaining more, or adding x's and o's. But instead I just write:

I'm sorry.

17

THE NEXT MORNING, I'm brewing a pot of Terry's imported coffee when there's a knock at the door. I shuffle down the hall in my jersey bathrobe and peer through the stained-glass window. Ray stands on the deck, a small brown bag clutched in his giant fist.

"Thanks," I say as he passes me the bag. I peer inside at the gooey pile of doughnuts. "Want to stay for one? Promise I won't tell."

Ray smiles and shakes his head. "K2 gets lonely." He shrugs back toward the car in the road. "We're listening to an audiobook. He's on a Dickens kick." He rolls his eyes and hops back down the steps, lumbering down the driveway.

I texted him early this morning out of desperation. I wasn't sure that breakfast treats and Terry's coffee were going to be enough to turn things around with Tess, but I knew I had to do something. I tossed and turned all night, replaying in my head all of what happened. When I decided to tell Sammy and Tess the truth about Noel, I knew they would be disappointed. But with Tess, it feels like something more. And she's not one to "talk things out." There's only guessing what's wrong, and doing whatever can be done to fix it.

Usually, this involves doughnuts. Every morning at camp there were doughnuts. Tess knew where they were kept in the kitchen and how to sneak in. Whenever one of us was down, or she was feeling city-sick, Tess would round us up for a late-night rendezvous, and we'd tiptoe down the woodchip-covered trail and stuff our faces in the dark with sticky, glazed goodness.

I stand at the stove, boiling water for tea—I've never been a coffee drinker, I'm jittery enough on my own—and I remember what Tess said about this summer. She thought it should be for us now what camp was for us then. Suddenly, I understand why that could never happen. There were no boys at camp.

It's hard to imagine now, after years of serial dating and ping-ponging from one long-term relationship to the next, but when I was younger, boys were never on my radar. Or, I should say, I wasn't on theirs. I'd get jealous, sometimes, about the way guys always waited for Sammy outside after junior high, showing off and acting like morons, fighting for her attention. In high school, it was clear that Sammy was on the fast track to popularity—captain of the dance team, prom queen, the works—while I was still going fishing with Gramps and goofing around on my guitar. But by that point, Sammy was too loyal to set me free. Sometimes I think she's the only reason I got out of that place alive. Sammy, and writing music.

Tess was different. I could sense that she needed us, from the very first day of camp, even if she didn't immediately agree. She mentioned her parents' recent divorce only to say that getting rid of her for the summer was the first thing they'd agreed on in years. By the end of that first summer, Tess had dragged us out on all kinds of late-night adventures, and gotten us into more trouble than we ever would have found on our own. She replaced every Top 40 song on my iPod with obscure indie bands, and to this day, any cool cred I may have earned in my life or my music, I owe almost entirely to her. She's a big part of the reason I moved to New York. I knew I wanted her by my side, physically and emotionally, for as long as she could handle being there. Which is why I can't let her stay mad at me for long. No matter how badly I screw up, Sammy and I have too much history for her to ever give up on me. But with Tess, I'm not so sure.

The kettle whistles and I pour a cup of tea for me, a mug of rich-smelling coffee for Tess. I arrange a pile of doughnuts on a dainty floral plate, and balance the whole spread on a tray, then pad carefully up the creaky steps. I knock gently on Tess's door.

Nothing.

I open the door a crack. She's sprawled on top of the quilt, her dark curls piled over her face. "Tess?" I whisper. "Are you awake?"

Tess grunts and rolls over. I edge the tray onto the wicker bedside table. "I brought you something," I say, nudging her shoulder.

Tess inches toward the wall and tosses the quilt over her head.

"Doughnuts!" I announce cheerily. "I know they're not Krispy Kreme, but they look pretty authentic. Cinnamon glazed . . . Your favorite."

Tess doesn't move. I watch the bulge of blankets rise and fall with her breathing.

"Real coffee, too," I try. "It smells amazing. Here."

I waft the steam from the tray over in her general direction, but Tess continues to ignore me. Finally, I throw up my hands. "Come on!" I erupt. "I'm trying! I said I was sorry. You have to give me something!"

Tess whips the quilt from her shoulders and spins around to face me on the bed. "Give you something?" she spits back at me. "I give you everything! I work for you! I live with you! I do everything for you. Everything I have, everything I do, revolves around you. Is it too much to ask for something to be *just mine*?"

She stares at me, breathing heavily, sleep still stuck to the corners of her eyes. I sit, frozen, stunned and confused.

"Noel?" I finally ask. "But . . ."

"Ugh!" Tess groans, picking up a pillow and aggressively flopping it into my lap. "Not Noel! Not everything is about a *guy*, you know . . ."

"I know," I say defensively. "I just don't know what else I did wrong."

"You didn't *do* anything wrong," she says. "That's the point. You don't do anything, and still, it's like, just by being here, you make everything different."

I sigh, a strange sadness settling around my heart. It's the same old story, the never-ending balancing act that has become my life. "Oh. That."

I used to spend a lot of time worrying about how being around me was affecting my family and friends. At first, of course, all the attention, the fame, was exciting for all of us. But it wasn't long before the newness wore off, and I could tell it was a struggle. It's been hard for me, too, but I signed up for this. They didn't. That's why being on the island, for me, has felt like a magical escape. I feel it changing me, slowly breaking down the walls I've been so carefully building. But I've never stopped to think about how *I* might be changing *it*.

"I'm sorry," I say. "I know this was your place."

Tess pulls the quilt into her lap, picking at the worn corners. "It was the only thing that always stayed the same. Every time I came back, no matter what else was going on, at school, my parents . . ."

I peer through the curtains of Tess's crazy curls and see the same girl I met that first day of camp. No matter how much she complained about the early morning wake-up calls, the heat, the bugs, the silly camp uniform we had to wear on Sundays, we always knew the four weeks we spent there were her favorite four weeks of the year. We knew because it was the same for us, too.

"I know," I say. I want to say more. I want to say that sometimes I hate all of the attention, too. But complaining about this life, this ridiculous, privileged, anything-is-possible life, always makes me feel uneasy. Like it might be snatched up, taken away in an instant, and I'd be left the same awkward girl I used to be, stuck in the middle of nowhere, dreaming. So instead, all I say is, "I'm sorry."

Tess picks up the pillow and bats me with it again, playfully this time. "Me too," she says. "I didn't mean what

I said about bringing you here. I'm sorry I'm such a brat."

"You can't help it." I shrug playfully, handing her the plate of doughnuts. "It's all you know."

Tess nods earnestly and takes the plate into her lap. She peers at the doughnuts, gingerly picking one up and taking a bite. "Imposter," she rules, dropping it back onto the plate with a *thud*.

I laugh and pass her the coffee. She takes a careful sip.

"Better?" I ask.

"Anything would be better than the watery junk they sell in town," she says, taking another sip. "Are you going to see him again?"

"Who?"

Tess rolls her eyes. "'*Who?*'" she mocks me, feigning innocence.

There's a tightness around my heart as I remember the text I sent last night. "I don't think so," I say at last. I know it wasn't my seeing Noel that upset Tess, but I also know that he's a part of what makes this place so special to her. There isn't a lot that happened in her childhood that she remembers fondly. I can't ruin this for her.

"Oh, don't be an idiot," Tess says. "I want you to see him."

"You do?"

Tess nods, licking her fingers.

"But what about all that stuff you said? I need to stop

losing myself in relationships. I'm not ready."

Tess shrugs. "You're probably not," she says. "But so what? This is who you are, Bird. It's the reason people who have never met you send you holiday cards, and knit your face into sweaters, and light candles for you at church. They love your music, yes, but they also love *you*. Like, really love you. And it's because they know you care about them. You care about everyone. You'd fall in love with a paper bag if it hung around you long enough."

I laugh, pressing the corners of my eyes to keep the tears from leaking out. "I just feel like I'm always letting you guys down," I say. "I'm afraid I'll screw things up again, and next time, you won't be there. I'm worried you'll give up on me."

"Give up on you?" Tess looks at me like I'm speaking in tongues. "You're the only reason I'm here right now. You cared about me when nobody else did. When my own parents couldn't stand to be around me. I did everything to get you to leave me alone, and you wouldn't."

Tess pauses, her eyes glassy. The only time I've ever seen her cry was when she rode her fixed-gear bike into the open door of a garbage truck and cracked two ribs. She sniffles, looks away, and swats at her face with both hands. "There aren't enough bonehead boyfriends in the world to make me give up on you."

I lean my head on her shoulder. She lets me cuddle

for a second before straightening and stretching for her coffee on the table.

I shift on the bed and reach into the pocket of my bathrobe for my phone.

"What are you doing?" she asks.

I scroll through my contacts and find Noel's name. My thumb is poised over the red Delete Contact button.

"Don't do that!" Tess squeals. "I told you, I don't care."

"I know," I say. "But I do." I press the button.

Are you sure you want to delete this contact? the phone asks.

In a flash, I see Noel's face. I remember the way he looked when I left him, after another night on the water. I caught him watching me walk away and he'd pretended he was searching for Murphy in the dunes. My heart clenches at the idea that it could be the last time I see him. It feels impossible that I won't even get to say a real good-bye.

But not as impossible as losing Tess.

I press the button—*Yes*—and tuck the phone back into my pocket. There's a sad tug on my heart, but I breathe through it. It's for the best. I need to get back to work anyway. No excuses. No distractions. Even if it means no Noel.

Tess shakes her head. "Lily Ross, breaking hearts and taking names."

I roll my eyes. "Better me than them." I jump off her bed and scrounge around in the messy top drawer of her dresser. "Now hurry up."

"Where are we going?" Tess asks, lowering her feet to the floor and stretching her arms to the ceiling.

I find her bathing suit and toss it onto her lap. "We're going to the beach," I say. "Because we're on vacation. And those waves aren't going to surf themselves."

18

52 Days Until Tour
July 22nd

TESS TRUDGES TO the shore with her surfboard, dropping it with a heavy *thud* onto the pebbled beach. "And that's a wrap." It's been almost a week since I brought her doughnuts and dragged her into the water, surf gear in tow, and very little progress has been made.

To Tess's credit, the waves haven't exactly been cooperating; they're either too small, or too big and sloppy, or they're breaking too far out. As a show of solidarity, I've paddled out once or twice, zipping myself into her rented wet suit and splashing through face-fulls of whitecaps. I stood up on the board once, but just long enough to see a rock in my direct path, panic, and tumble off gracelessly.

"You're giving up?" Sammy asks, her book spread open on her lap. She refuses to go swimming—Sammy's afraid of sharks, an excuse she's been using since the water safety class we had to take in the notably shark-free lake at camp—and instead has spent the week working her way through her romance novel. "But it's your summer goal!"

"Don't talk to me about goals, Speed Reader." Tess slaps her towel at Sammy's ankles. "You've been buried in that book for weeks. How are you possibly not finished?"

"I have bad eyesight," Sammy says, pulling her reading glasses out of her hair.

Tess laughs. "I've heard those work better when you actually wear them."

It's a good question, actually—Sammy has been spending a lot of time on a book she hasn't seemed to have made much of a dent in. She's never been a big reader, but I'd know if my best friend was illiterate, right? I wave off Tess's teasing, though, not wanting Sam to feel embarrassed.

"Ladies," I intervene. "This is supposed to be fun. Nobody has to surf—or read—if they don't want to." I try not to sound smug, though I'm secretly proud of my own recent progress. In the last week, I've written two more Noel-free songs and proven to myself, once and for all, that my talent is not inseparably linked to whichever member of the male species I've temporarily decided is "the one."

"Thanks, Mom," Tess sings. She dries off her hands and reaches into the pocket of Sammy's bag for her phone, glances quickly at the time. "I have to get ready."

"Ready for what?" I ask.

"Yoga," Tess answers, reaching around to unzip the back of her wet suit.

"You're going again?" Sammy asks.

The three of us have been back to Maya's Saturday morning yoga class twice, but lately Tess has been finding other classes to attend on her own. Tess is notoriously against any kind of organized group activity, particularly those involving exercise, so her newfound commitment to down dogs and warriors has raised a few eyebrows around here.

"I like it." Tess peels off the thick layers of her wet suit and leaves it in a wrinkled heap on the sand. "And we're not exactly overbooked."

"I think it's great," I say, smiling at her.

"Meet you back at the house," Tess says. "What time's dinner?"

"Whenever we want." With more songs under my belt, I've decided to switch gears and work on my other summer goal: cooking. The fact that it also distracts me from thinking about Noel is just an added bonus.

After deleting his number, I expected it wouldn't be long until I heard from him, and I spent many nights lying awake, imagining how I'd explain myself when I did. But he never called, or texted, and even though I was the one who'd made the decision to lie low, I found myself getting frustrated that he wasn't trying harder. Hadn't he wondered why I didn't show up on the beach that night? Didn't he even care?

Sammy and I make our way lazily back to the house, and while she showers I text K2 and ask him to run me into town. Tonight I'm making my favorite: linguini in clam sauce. We picked up most of the groceries earlier in the week but I figured I'd save the seafood for last.

The fish market is at one end of Main Street, tucked against the harbor. It's bustling with activity, fishermen hauling in the day's catch through the back door, and shoppers standing in a line that snakes through the front. The people waiting are a mix of day-trippers, waiting to take photos of themselves with a live lobster, and islanders picking up fish for dinner. Noel taught me to recognize the difference: Day-trippers usually wear shoes and carry purses. Locals wear flip-flops, when they wear shoes at all, and tend to pay on credit.

I shuffle inside the cozy shop. Deep coolers stacked with shellfish and fillets line the walls, and a big chalkboard advertises the day's offerings and prices.

I scan a nearby refrigerator and choose a few dips and spreads, balancing them in a Tupperware tower as I head toward the register. One of the plastic containers topples to the ground, rolling along the floor and stopping at the feet of an older man.

"Here you go," he says as he passes the container ahead to me in line. He has a scruffy gray beard and studies me with kind eyes. "Hey! Aren't you that gal on the radio? The one my granddaughter is so nuts about?"

I smile and rearrange my pile. The people in line between us stop their conversations and a hush falls over the busy room. "I sure hope so."

The man beams. "What the hell are you doing out here?" he asks to the amusement of the growing crowd. "Don't they have fish out in California?"

"Not like this, they don't!" A woman behind the counter breaks in, holding up two enormous lobsters and tossing them into a cooler in the back.

"She doesn't care about your sea rats," the man says, cutting the line to stage-whisper to me. "You ever want a real meal, you come to my house. I make the best fish stew on the island." He taps my elbow with two arthritic fingers.

"Is that right?"

I realize how good it feels to be interacting with people again. This is the longest I've gone without doing an event or making an appearance—even an informal one like going out to lunch or surprising a fan club—and I hadn't realized how much I'd missed feeling connected.

"Keep it moving, George," a familiar voice interrupts from just beyond the back door. "Or I'll tell Louise you've been flirting again."

I turn to see Noel dropping a heavy cooler on the dock behind the market. Our eyes meet for a quick moment and he nods, then walks back out to his boat.

"You tell her!" George shouts. "She could use a little competition."

Laughter fills the market and George offers to buy me my clams. I decline, but promise to try his famous stew one day, and take a few photos with twin girls and their shoe-wearing parents, visiting from Montreal.

After I've paid, I sneak through the back door and glance around the dock for Noel.

I find his boat docked near the fuel pump, and see him huddled together with Latham and J.T. They're busy unloading traps and gear, and I wait for the guys to leave, shuttling coolers back to the fish market. I take a breath and walk out onto the pier, the uneven wooden decking creaking beneath my feet.

Murphy sees me first. He races toward me, his tail wagging ferociously. I scratch behind his ears and keep walking, his nose nudging the side of my knee.

"Hey," I call out. Noel's back is to me on the boat and he doesn't turn around. I feel my face getting hot—is he really going to ignore me?—until I notice the white cord of his earbuds running from his ears to his pocket.

I grab on to one of the tall wooden pylons and lean into the boat, tapping Noel on the shoulder. He jumps slightly and plucks the earbuds from his ears.

"Anything good?" I ask him as he stashes his phone in his pocket. My arms are folded tightly across my chest and I can feel my heart beating against my wrist, so intensely that I worry it may be shaking the whole boat.

"Just your average clown rap." It's a joke, but his eyes aren't smiling. They look tired, their usual sparkle flattened and dull. "Hope George wasn't giving you too much of a hard time in there."

"Not at all. He seemed sweet."

"He's a troublemaker." We stand for a few moments in quiet before he clears his throat. "How have you been? Good?"

"Really good," I say, my voice strained and too loud. "Everything's great. I just . . . you know . . . I wanted to apologize for the other night."

He keeps busy as I'm talking, hopping onto the dock and uncoiling a long, damp rope. I'm not sure why I feel the need to lie to him, to make it seem like I haven't missed him every second of every day. I lean heavily into the pillar.

"The other night?" he asks distractedly.

"At the beach," I say, my face flushing. He bends down to loop the rope around a metal cleat. "And for not calling. It's been . . . things have been kind of crazy."

He inches by me, our shoulders bumping as he passes. A shock of electricity runs through me and I want more than anything to touch him, to hug him, to sit on the boat beside him and steam off toward the horizon. I take a deep breath. "I've been doing a lot of writing," I say. "And hanging out with my friends. You know, that's really why I came out here. It was supposed to be this, like, bonding trip, and so, I don't know, I guess I just decided that . . ."

Noel rummages loudly through the storage bench. He takes out a roll of paper towels and a spray bottle and starts to scrub the windows of the cockpit. The towels squeak across the glass in intense circles. "Can you please *stop*?" I finally shout.

Noel pauses mid-wipe and balls the towel up in his hand before tossing it into the back of the boat. With crossed arms, he sits down on top of the bench and chews the inside of one cheek.

I take a deep breath. "Sorry. I just . . . I'm trying to explain . . ."

He looks up at me abruptly. "Explain what?"

His voice is harsh. I feel flustered, and then annoyed. Why is he making this so difficult?

"Look," he says, leaning forward to rest his elbows on his knees. "You don't have to do this."

"I don't?"

He shakes his head. "No. I get it. It's not like I thought this was a real *thing*, or whatever. I know you're busy. And I'm . . ." He gestures out to the water. "I'm here. It's fine. It is what it is."

I stare at him. There's so much I want to say that it feels like the words are trampling over each other, tumbling around and getting mixed up. I want to tell him that this week has felt like an eternity, that it's taken every ounce of willpower I have not to call him. That going to the beach with my friends has been torture because every time I see the water I think of him. I want to tell him that I don't want to be busy. I want to be here, too.

But then I see the familiar shape of two girls walking along the pier in yoga clothes. It takes me a minute to realize that it's Tess and Maya, and they're laughing, each holding an ice cream cone. It's not until they get a few paces closer that I realize their free hands are clasped together between them.

"What's wrong?" Noel asks. I realize that my

mouth has dropped open. I'm frozen in place. *Tess and Maya?*

I keep watching as they pass the fish market. Maya looks out toward the water, squinting into the sun, and Tess turns, too.

Noel follows my silent gaze. "Is that Tess? Who is she with?"

"Our yoga teacher." I hold my hand over my head to wave, and watch Tess's eyes widen as she sees me. There's a moment where she looks like she wants to run away, her eyes darting frantically toward the parking lot, the water, searching for the quickest escape.

"That's Maya Scott," Noel says.

"You know her?"

He nods. "She was a grade above me. Valedictorian of her class. Way to go, Tess."

Tess holds Maya's hand tighter and together they walk toward us on the dock.

"Hey, Birdie. Noel." Tess greets him with a big smile, as if she'd planned the whole thing: running into the two of us together, being with Maya, all of it. "I was hoping to catch you guys."

"You were?" I eye her skeptically, before smiling at Maya. "How was class?"

"It was great," Maya says. "Even got this one to stay awake."

She nudges Tess playfully. Despite being caught off guard, Tess seems happy and calm in a way I haven't ever seen before.

Noel is back to tinkering with his boat and Tess looks from him to me, trying to telepathically communicate something. I shrug, not sure what she's asking, and she clears her throat.

"Noel, I don't know what Lily's told you, but I want to apologize," she says. I try to catch her eye again, to wordlessly communicate that it's not necessary, but she stares steadily at Noel. "I was . . . I was having a hard time with . . . lots of things . . . and I kind of freaked out. This place was always special to me . . ."

I glance at Maya and see her give Tess a reassuring smile. I can't be sure, but I have a strong suspicion she's heard at least part of this before. I feel a quick spike of jealousy, realizing that Tess has been confiding in someone else.

"You were part of that," Tess goes on. "And when Lily told me you guys were seeing each other, I think I was scared of losing it all. So if she's been weird . . . weirder than usual, I mean . . . it's my fault." She turns to me with a smile. "The truth is, I haven't seen her this happy, like, ever. And if, for some strange reason, that has something to do with you, how could I stand in the way?"

Noel blushes and looks down at the shifting slats

of the dock. My shoulders suddenly relax, a flood of warmth filling my body.

"And now that we've all survived my very first grown-up apology," Tess continues, "who wants to go surfing?" She looks from Noel to me, gently squeezing my elbow. "This girl is dying for a lesson."

Noel looks to me uncertainly. "Really?"

I beam. "Absolutely."

Noel jumps from the boat to the dock to stand beside me. I want to hug Tess, I want her to know how grateful I am, that she's opening up, not just to the idea that Noel truly makes me happy, but to the possibility of being happy with somebody, herself.

While the three of them are chatting, I notice the white tangle of Noel's earbuds dangling from his pocket, slipping toward the ocean.

"Careful," I say, quickly reaching for them. His phone tumbles out into my hands and I hear the soft, distant beat of music still playing through the tiny speakers. I glance at the screen of his phone and see the cover of my last album staring back at me.

Perfect red circles bloom on his cheeks and he stuffs the phone back into his pocket.

"Clown rap, huh?" I whisper.

He shrugs and takes my hand, and suddenly, everything feels right again.

19

THE NEXT DAY, Noel offers to take us all out on his boat to a nearby island, a local surf spot that's apparently so secret it doesn't have a name. "We just call it 'off-shore,'" explains J.T., zipping into his wet suit on the dark and pebbly sand once we've docked. I should be working on the last few songs for the album, but somehow it's starting to feel less important. Now that I'm back with Noel, summer is winding down too fast. Maybe Terry is right—maybe I won't push it. Maybe I'll just release the tour EP, a special gift for my fans.

"Off-shore" turns out to be an uninhabited island, thickly settled with looming evergreens and acres of brambly shrubs. Rolling waves break in a steady line parallel with the short, secluded beach. As soon as Latham has slathered on some sunscreen, he and J.T. belly-flop onto their boards and start paddling out away from land, their arms digging into the water in long, determined strokes.

"Ready?" Noel asks Tess, who has agreed to be his first student. Sammy and I bring beach chairs and towels to a sandy spot near the dunes, and I rummage through my tote for sunglasses.

"Ready for my daily near-drowning?" Tess shoots back, with an overly enthusiastic thumbs-up. "You bet!"

We offer calls of encouragement as Tess wobbles onto her board, and Noel follows her out toward where the waves are breaking. Murphy paddles alongside them for a few feet before losing interest and turning back to join us, panting heavily as he cools off in the sand beside us.

In the distance, Noel has stopped Tess in a calm section of the cove and they practice getting into position. Noel stands waist-deep beside her, keeping the board steady, and Tess lies flat on her belly with her toes pointing back. When Noel shouts "Go!" she assumes push-up stance, hops her feet to the middle of the board, and twists to the side, one foot forward and the other straddled back.

Sammy and I cheer wildly and Tess turns to us, losing focus and tumbling backward into the shallow sea. Noel shakes his head and gestures for Tess to follow him out deeper, where they can work undisturbed.

"She seems so happy." Sammy smiles at the closed book in her lap. From the dog-eared page in the middle, it looks like she still hasn't made much progress.

"I know," I say, rubbing sunscreen on my arms. "It's weird."

Sammy laughs and fidgets in her chair, adjusting the seam of her black-and-white polka-dotted bandeau top. "You do, too. Noel is really sweet."

There's a fluttering near my heart, the slightly embarrassing, gushy feeling I get whenever I see Noel or so much as hear his name. I reach down to pat the coarse wet fur beneath Murphy's collar. "He is," I say, hearing the dreamy quality in my voice. I clear my throat, weirdly self-conscious, and study the chipped red polish on my fingernails. I feel Sammy's eyes on me and worry that there's something new and almost uncomfortable between us.

For most of our lives, Sam has been the one person I've always been able to be myself around. Even when everyone else thought I was too intense, always writing or singing or talking about writing and singing, she made me feel like I was special. She promised that one day, everyone else would see it, too. I figured that when I came clean about Noel, things would go back to the way they'd always been, that whatever tension I'd been feeling between us would lift because there were no secrets anymore. But it's still there, this awkward delay between the things we want to say and the things we're actually saying, and I don't know what to do about it.

"I hate that I lied to you," I blurt, a pressure in my jaw, too-late tears stinging the corners of my eyes.

"I know," Sammy says. "It's okay."

"It's not okay," I insist. "It was stupid. I was just . . . I was scared. I didn't want you guys to tell me I was making another mistake."

"I wouldn't have said it was a mistake . . ." Sam digs at the sand with her bare heels.

I study her disbelievingly until she relents.

"Fine." She holds up her hands. "I may have *gently reminded* you that the whole point of this summer was to spend time on your own. But that doesn't excuse the fact that you lied."

"I know it doesn't," I say softly. "I hate when you're mad at me. It makes my stomach hurt."

"I'm not mad at you," she insists. "I can never stay mad at you."

I laugh abruptly. "Remember when I had that audition and missed your Halloween party?" I ask. "You made me wear a different costume every time I came over until Christmas!"

"That's true," Sam admits, her eyes taking on a faraway look as she thinks back to a simpler time, a time when all we had to worry about were rides to the mall and multiple-choice tests. "But I wasn't mad."

We turn our attention back to the ocean, where Tess and Noel are sitting up on their boards, their legs dangling in the water. Every so often, Noel turns his head to check for incoming waves. Latham and J.T. are floating blobs of color on the horizon, bobbing in the growing swell.

Sammy fidgets again with her book and clears her throat. It looks like there's more she wants to ask, or say. I realize with a guilty shock that maybe she has something else on her mind. Maybe whatever it is that's bothering her has nothing at all to do with me.

"What about you?" I ask, hoping for a convincing mix of casual and concerned. "Are you having an okay time? I know things have been a little . . . slow here."

Sammy shrugs and bites her lower lip, a dead giveaway that something is up. "No, it's great," she tries. "I mean, yeah, I'm a little . . . I don't know . . . I guess I'm just feeling antsy with all of this downtime. But I think it's good for me, you know? The quiet. It really makes you figure things out."

"Tell me about it," I say, and we laugh, the easy sparkle back in her emerald eyes.

Just then, Noel shouts something in the water and we

turn to see a perfect wave taking shape in the distance. Noel is miming furiously at Tess, who stares wide-eyed in our direction, her strong arms slicing into the ocean again and again. The wave grows behind her, a lip of white breaking on one side and slowly spreading, like whipped cream on a warm pie just before it melts.

"Now!" Noel yells, and in one expert motion Tess pops up to her feet. The wave chases her from behind, pushing her down the line for a breathtaking few seconds. Her back is hunched and her knees are bent, but just before she topples over, she pumps one fist in the air, whooping proudly at the sky.

In the afternoon, after we've all had our turns in the water, our arms sore from paddling, our hair damp and threaded with sand, Noel sneaks me off to a tucked-away swimming hole connected to the beach by an overgrown trail.

It's much smaller than the one he showed me on the main island but twice as deep. Noel dives in first and I follow, swimming out to meet him. The sunlight is broken by branches into dappled patches and the air is cool and crisp, but Noel's arms are warm as he pulls me in close.

"Think they're having fun?" he asks, nodding his head back to the beach. His blue eyes are genuine and concerned. It's the first time we've all been together since I told Sammy and Tess about us, and I realize he's feeling a new sense of pressure, a need to prove himself as worthy, even though he's known Tess longer than I have.

"It's the perfect day," I assure him. "Thank you."

Noel kisses my nose and tenderly pushes my wet hair out of my face, before picking me up by the waist and tossing me brusquely into the water. I shriek and splash up to the surface, determined to get him back. We laugh and wrestle, attempting to climb whatever body parts we can get ahold of, pushing each other down and calling false truces again and again.

Eventually, we flop back onto the sun-warmed ledge and lie on our backs, my head resting on Noel's chest. I trace lines on his tanned forearm with my finger.

"Why 'Bird'?" he asks suddenly, tucking my damp hair behind one ear.

"What do you mean?" I prop myself up on one elbow. "My nickname?"

Noel nods, stretching his arms overhead and resting his head on his open palms. "Who gets to use it?" he asks. "Is there some kind of initiation? A secret handshake?"

I laugh and snuggle back in, my forehead pressed against the stubbly side of his jaw. "Tess started it," I explain. "It's mostly just for family and close friends.

But I could make an exception . . ." I tilt my head to smile up at him.

"Nah." He shrugs. "I like Lily. Lily Ross," he says, landing on each syllable with warm precision. There's something about the way he says my name, my real name, that makes it sound new again, somehow unattached to the *Lily Ross* I've been trying to separate myself from all summer. It doesn't sound like a business. It sounds like a real person.

Like me.

"Do you ever think about what happens after?" he asks, shifting slightly against the hard rocks. His voice is light but his heart pounds behind his ribs, drumming against my outstretched fingers.

"After what?" I ask, looking over the feathery tops of the trees, at a wispy trail of clouds that snakes across the sky.

"When you're done with all of this," Noel says, locking his fingers into mine. "Touring. Traveling. You can't do it forever, can you?"

I look at the web of our fingers, mine long and slender, his thick and calloused. "I don't know," I say softly. "To be honest, I've always thought I would."

He laughs, nervously. "But now?"

I smile. "Now I'm not so sure," I say. "It's hard to see when you're in the middle of it, and most of the time I just feel so lucky, you know? But it does seem like there's a lot you miss out on, living that way."

"Oh yeah?" He sits up slowly, and I lift my head. A slight smile is spreading hesitantly across his face. "Like what?"

"Oh, I don't know," I tease, shifting to sit beside him. "Lots of things."

Noel scrambles to his feet and starts to climb back up the trail, disappearing around a tree. "Where are you going?" I call after him. He doesn't answer, and I follow the rustling sound of his feet in the bushes until he reappears high on another clearing.

At the top of the cliff, he peers through a cluster of trees, struggling to untangle something. When he returns, he's dragging a long, sturdy rope, tied to a thick branch overhead.

"What are you doing?" I yell, laughing. "That thing looks like it's been there since the Middle Ages."

Noel gives it a good tug. "Yup," he agrees. "Entertaining bored island youth for centuries."

He beckons me to join him but I shake my head. "No way."

Noel shrugs dramatically. "Suit yourself!" He steps out to the ledge, and jumps up and down a few times while holding the rope, as if to prove that it's up to the task. Finally he backs up, then careens in a careful arc over the water, dropping the rope from his grasp. He pulls his knees tidily into his chest and spins backward in an impressive double flip, before slicing into the water in a flawless dive.

I wait until he splashes through the surface and cheer loudly from the lower ledge. Noel runs a hand through his hair, pressing short, choppy blond strands back from his face, and gives me a mischievous smile. "Come on," he goads. "You're not scared, are you?"

I glance up at the steep rock face and the fraying length of rope. It's the kind of thing I'd normally shy away from, not because I don't want to do it, but for fear of being photographed in an awkward position, or ending up with some kind of stupid injury that would be a nightmare to explain. But there are no cameras here. For once, I don't have to think beyond this moment. I don't have to worry that whatever happens will get twisted, revised, rewritten, until it no longer belongs to me.

I push myself onto the lower ledge and climb up. At the top, I unravel the rope and give it a steady tug.

My stomach drops as I peer over the edge, considering the distance. Noel cups his hands around his mouth and yells something up to me, but it's swallowed in echoes and I can't quite make it out.

"What?" I yell back.

"Jump and I'll tell you!"

I roll my eyes and take a deep breath, the rough fibers of the rope digging into my palms. Before I can change my mind, I back up, then run to the ledge and swing out over the water. Just as I let the rope slip from my fingers, falling weightless and free, the trees a blanket of green around me, I hear Noel's voice:

"I'm falling for you, Lily Ross!"

The water races to meet me, a breath-snatching barrier of cold, but I'm smiling as I sink down beneath the surface. I squint my eyes open, kicking toward the milky light. When I break the surface, Noel is a few feet away, beaming. I paddle closer and wrap my arms around his neck.

"You're crazy," I whisper into the warm side of his rough cheek. "And I'm falling for you, too."

20

48 Days Until Tour
July 26th

NOEL'S HOUSE IS actually three houses. Four, if you count the chicken coop. After a few days of hanging out at our place—more surf sessions with Noel on our beach, yoga with Maya on the deck, long, festive dinners, and lots and lots of board games—I decide to surprise Noel at home. It's the first night we haven't spent together all week, and I consider calling or texting first, but I'm feeling adventurous, and proud that—with a little help from Tess—I've managed to find him on my own. She gave me general directions, whatever she remembered from when she used to play there as a kid, and K2 and I drive slowly around the neighborhood until I spy a red mailbox in the shape of a boat, with BRADLEY painted in black on both sides.

K2 leaves me at the end of a long, shell-covered driveway, and I crunch uncertainly toward a cluster of small houses. One of them is clearly the main house, with a covered porch and a pile of rubber boots angled near the door. Another is a smaller shack, with a clothesline hanging from one window and rigged to the top of an outdoor shower. A third looks like a toolshed and is packed with gear; rusted beach chairs, old surfboards, and an ancient-looking lawn mower spill out onto the patchy lawn.

The chickens are loose, and a few of them scurry over, trailing me to the front door.

As I get closer I hear the clank and sizzle of cooking sounds, water running, the chatter of televised sports. The front door is wedged open and I rap on it lightly, peering across a tiled floor to the living room, where a pair of bare feet is elevated at one end of a worn, leather couch.

"Hello?" I call out.

There's a patter of footsteps and the door opens wider, revealing a girl of about fourteen. Her blond hair is pulled back into a thick ponytail, and she wears cutoff jean shorts and a gray sweatshirt with a pink robot on it. When she sees me, she whispers, her lips barely moving:

"*Oh my God.*"

I smile and hold up my hand in a wave. "Hi. You must be Sidney. I'm Lily. Is Noel around?"

She stands frozen in the doorway, her mouth hanging slightly open. "Oh my God. Oh my God," she says again, this time a bit louder. "Wait. Don't move. I think . . ." She closes her eyes for a second, then snaps them open again, holding one hand to her stomach. "I thought I might puke. You know that feeling you get when you think you're going to puke but then you don't puke? That happened. But I think it's passing." She takes a deep breath. "Yup. I'm good."

I laugh. "That's good."

"Yeah. Good." Sidney nods seriously. "Come in. Do you want to come in? Or not. Whatever. NOEL!" She erupts suddenly, screaming Noel's name without taking her eyes off of me, as if she's afraid I might vanish. "NOEL!"

"What in the hell?" I hear Noel from the kitchen. The faucet turns off and he rushes toward the door. "What is wrong with you— Oh," he says, clearly taken aback. His eyes flit quickly from my face to the house around him, and his cheeks redden. "Did we . . . did we have plans?"

I feel my smile slipping and clear my throat. He looks shocked, and not in a totally comfortable way. Maybe this was a mistake. "No," I say. "I thought I'd surprise you. But I can go, I mean, if it's not a good time . . ."

"No!" Sidney yells. "It's a fine time! The finest of times! I don't know why I'm yelling. Am I yelling?"

"Sid." Noel puts a hand on her shoulder. "Maybe you want to go tell Dad we have company?" He nods toward the living room.

"Sure," Sidney says, but doesn't make a move.

"Now?" Noel presses, physically shifting her out of the doorway and ushering me inside. "Sorry about her," he says softly as I pass. "I'd say she's not usually like this, but . . . she is."

I smile and pretend not to listen to the conversation happening in frantic whispers over my shoulder. The TV switches off and there are more shuffling footsteps. "Here we go . . ." Noel says under his breath, almost to himself.

Sidney reappears, dragging a man in flannel pajama pants and a black T-shirt behind her. His face is an older, more rugged version of Noel's: the same clear blue eyes and strong jaw. He holds out a hand and smiles warmly. "Hello," he says. "My daughter says I'm not allowed to talk to you. I'm Lew."

"Lewis," Sidney interrupts. "His real name is Lewis. It's a family name."

"Hi, Lew," I say as he shakes my hand firmly. "I'm Lily. It's not a family name. My mom just liked the flower."

"It's a beautiful flower." Lew smiles. "A beautiful flower for a beautiful girl!"

"Dad!" Sidney clutches the sides of her head like her brain might leak out. "That's disgusting! I told you not to say anything. Does he have to be here?" Sid turns pleadingly to Noel.

"Yes, he has to be here," Noel says. "Sid, Dad, why don't you guys finish watching the game, and Lily and I will make dinner. Sound good?"

"I thought you'd never ask." Lew smiles pleasantly and shuffles back into the living room. "Let's go, Sid. I'll give you the big chair so you can eavesdrop."

"I wasn't going to eavesdrop," Sidney whines, following her father reluctantly.

Noel puts his hand on the small of my back and leads me into the kitchen. The sink is stacked with dirty dishes and the countertops are covered in mixing bowls. A thick slab of white fish is on a plate near the stove, next to a box of Ritz crackers.

"Sorry about the mess," Noel says. "I'm kind of a disaster in the kitchen."

"What's for dinner?" I ask, before whispering: "Are you sure this is all right?"

Noel holds my chin in one hand and plants a quick kiss on my lips. "I'm sure," he says. "If you'd told me you were coming I could have prepared them a little. And you."

"Prepare me? For what?" I watch as Noel takes out a roll of crackers and begins to pound it against the countertop.

"My dad's lame jokes," he says, crunching the crackers into a fine dust. "Sid being . . . Sid."

"I wanted to meet your family." There's an unopened globe of Brussels sprouts on the table and I start to peel back the plastic. "Not your *prepared* family. What are you doing?"

Noel pours the cracker crumbs into a bowl. "Making bread crumbs," he says, eyeing the big box of crackers. "What, they don't do it like this in New York?"

I laugh, holding out my hand as he passes me a knife. We work together in the kitchen, settling into an easy rhythm as we chop, peel, mix, and clean. It's funny to think that this would've been hard for me just a few months ago, but my cooking goals have really paid off. It feels effortless and fun, but maybe some of that is Noel, and the way he makes everything feel so easy.

Sid spends dinner either peppering me with questions (everything from "If you could only listen to one song on repeat for the rest of your life, what would it be?" to "Do you believe in aliens?") or watching me chew in a stunned silence. There's something so earnest and familiar about her that I like her right away, but it's not until we're in the kitchen alone together, cleaning up the dishes, that I realize why. She is exactly the way I was at her age: passionate and awkward, confident and shy, all at the same time.

"Wanna see my room?" Sid asks when we're done with the dishes.

"I thought you'd never ask." I follow her up the stairs. Noel gives me a questioning look from the dining room table and I wave and mouth silently, *I'm fine*.

Sid takes the steps three at a time and leads me down a long hall. There's a gallery of photos on the hallway walls: Sid and Noel on the beach as kids, Noel and his dad on the boat, a black-and-white photo of a much younger Lew with a beautiful pregnant woman, a tiny, towheaded Noel grabbing on to her leg.

At the end of the hall is Sid's room, a small, low-ceilinged space. "This is it," Sid says, holding out her arm as I pass through the door. "Bed. Table. Lamp." She points to the furniture in the room, pausing at a collection of stuffed animals spilling out of a box on the floor. "Miscellany. Sorry it's a mess. I'm usually fairly organized, but I've been busy working on this project for class . . ."

She sits at the makeshift desk in the corner.

"What's the class?" I ask, scanning her bookshelves and noting all the familiar titles: *Anne of Green Gables*, Harry Potter, *Alice's Adventures in Wonderland*. Long after Sammy and everyone at school had made the shift to "cooler" books and TV, I was still stuck on the classics.

"It's a computer programming class at the community college," she says. "I do it online. We're building websites, front to back. I'm making one for my dad."

Her voice gets higher and faster as she starts explaining something about writing code, and my eyes wander to a bulletin board on the wall over her head. It's plastered in postcards from all over the world—Sri Lanka, Budapest, New Zealand, Rome. Beside it is a giant map with red thumbtacks stuck in various places.

"They're from my mom. She travels a lot. She's in Goa now. That's in India. It's in the southern part," she says, moving to the map. "Really beachy and beautiful. She says it's her favorite place to paint so far. The colors are so rich you can taste them."

I smile, watching as Sid checks the thumbtacks, making sure each one is secure. "Do you talk to her a lot?"

Sid shakes her head. "Just the postcards," she says. "Dad says it's expensive to call."

"You must miss her." I can't imagine not being able to call my mom—or to have been without her at Sid's age.

Sid shrugs. "Yeah," she says. "It was worse before Noel came home. Now we're okay. We take turns cooking, doing the laundry. Dad's really bad at that stuff. He can barely use the microwave without setting something on fire."

"I heard that," Lew yells from downstairs.

Sid rolls her eyes. "He built this house himself in the seventies. It's insulated with newspaper," she whispers. "No privacy."

"The house I grew up in was just like this," I say. "Well, sort of. It was smaller, actually. I shared a room with my parents until I was eight."

"You did?" Sid asks, her eyes wide with disbelief.

I nod. "Then I moved down to the basement, which I loved. It was like my own apartment," I say. "Except I had to share it with my mom's exercise bike."

Sid kneels to point through a low half window. "That's Noel's shack," she says, pointing to the little house with the clothesline. "He moved out there when he came back. It used to be my mom's painting studio. He cleaned it up and put a mattress on the floor. It's pretty cozy."

I smile, trying not to feel sad about the idea of Noel sleeping on the floor in the room where his mom used to paint before she left them. I think of my own mother, of all the afternoons we spent together in the kitchen, doing my homework, singing along to the radio, watching sappy movies on her bed.

"All right, you two, enough yammering," Lew calls from downstairs. "It's time to get down to business."

"Business?" I ask.

"I was afraid of this," Sid muses, shaking her head

as she leads me back downstairs. She stops short on the landing and turns to whisper in my ear: "Listen, if you want to get out of here, just tell him you're having lady troubles. That's what I usually do."

I fight back a giggle and peer over her shoulder into the living room, where Lew is on his knees, opening a black case on the floor.

"Dad, can we maybe do this another time?" Noel asks. "We're sort of in a rush."

"What rush?" Lew asks, clicking open the metal latches. "You going fishing?"

"No, but—"

"But nothing," Lew interrupts. "Take a load off. Lily and me are gonna jam."

He pulls a short, rounded instrument from the case and fits the strap over his shoulder. "Is that a mandolin?" I ask in awe, reaching out to touch the smooth body, the old, rusted strings.

"See? I told you she'd be impressed," Lew says, sitting on the couch and starting to tune the strings, one at a time.

"Dad used to play in a bluegrass band," Sid tells me, standing in the hall, her face a muddled mixture of pride and embarrassment. "They opened once for Bob Seger."

"Pete Seeger!" Lew corrects. "It was at an anti-nuke rally over on the mainland. Really nice guy. 'This Land Is Your Land.' You know it?"

Lew plays a few chords and starts singing, his rough voice smoothing out into a sweet, clear tenor. I raise an impressed eyebrow at Noel, who is cringing by the door. I take a seat on the floor. It's a song I haven't sung or heard since music class in the fourth grade, but somehow I remember most of the lyrics.

Sid sits beside me and joins in, urging Noel with a kick to his ankles. Noel shakes his head and crosses his arms defiantly, but when I catch his eyes, they're smiling.

21

48 Days Until Tour
July 26th

AS NOEL TAKES the turn out of his driveway and we start down the main road, K2 pulls out from his hidden spot to follow close behind us. Lew insisted that Noel drive me home, despite repeated assurances that I could manage on my own. "I don't care what's 'in' these days," he'd said over dessert—defrosted frozen cream puffs and a pint of Ben & Jerry's. "This boy was raised with manners."

"Thanks for doing that," Noel says with a grateful sideways glance. "I knew Sid was going to geek out. But I hoped my dad would keep it together." At the door, Lew passed me a mix CD he'd made of all his favorite folk classics, each title written on the paper sleeve in tiny, deliberate print.

"They were great." I tap the CD lightly against my knee. "It's been a while since a guy made me a mix."

"Careful," Noel warns. "He's working up to asking if he can tour with you."

I stare ahead through the windshield. A light rain has started falling and the windshield wipers squawk eagerly across the glass. There's a flutter in my stomach as I think about tour. The summer days are passing in hectic clusters. Soon, it will be time to get back on the road. There's a part of me that misses working, performing, the comforting chaos of being in a new city every few nights. But it means leaving the island. Leaving Noel. The idea of not seeing him every day makes my heart lurch into my throat.

I reach for Noel's hand and stare at our fingers locked together over the console. We still haven't talked about what comes next, which, I've learned, is pretty much a way of life around here. When there are fish to be caught, fires to make, and houses to build, there isn't much time for worrying about things that haven't happened yet.

The truck slows as Noel turns down our driveway, bumping over the potholes, his tires splashing through muddy puddles on the road.

"You guys expecting visitors?" Noel asks suddenly. I follow his gaze into the darkness, where an unfamiliar sedan is parked in front of the house.

"No," I say. "Pull over." Noel edges the car to the side of the driveway, where we're hidden by underbrush. My pulse quickens and I reach for my phone. Whenever Ray nags me to lock up at night, I tease him for being paranoid. This place feels about as dangerous as a Disney movie. But now I'm glad the guys are close by.

K2 rumbles past us in the Escalade, his headlights lighting up the uneven shingles on the front of the house. We watch as he gets out of the car and walks deliberately around the sedan, checking the plate and peering inside the darkened windows.

Suddenly, a tall shadow moves near the front steps, and K2 hurries to cut him off. I squeeze Noel's hand harder, until the figure moves into the light and I can see his face clearly.

"Is that . . ." Noel starts.

"Jed?" I squint through the windshield, pulling my hand from Noel's and reaching to open the door.

"Wait—" Noel calls after me. I hurry out of the truck and walk quickly through the rain.

Jed and K2 are shaking hands when I reach them, chatting about the weather and the rambling journey from the city.

"What are you doing here?" I interrupt, my voice shrill and harsh. Jed looks at me, his wide, expectant smile faltering only slightly. K2 gives us a curt nod and retreats to the SUV.

"I tried texting, but you didn't answer," Jed says, his broad shoulders hunched against the rain. "And I know how much you love surprises." He holds his arms out wide, an uncharacteristically goofy smile spreading across his face. "Surprise!"

I stare at him, my brain racing to process his presence on this road, on these steps, on this island. He's wearing dark-wash jeans and a beige cardigan with a floppy cowl neck, his hair damp with rain but still arranged in a perfect wave across his forehead. As much as I want to feel nothing, my heart trips and races, an eager warmth spreading throughout my body. We're not standing in the rain. We're back on the big leather couch at his apartment, his long legs draped over mine, my hand in his hair, absently twirling that perfect wave while he hums a new melody.

"Everything okay?" I hear from over my shoulder. My eyes dart furtively to the damp ground. I hear Noel's footsteps behind us on the gravel.

Jed looks past me and I see his body shift, as if he's suddenly grown even taller. He extends his hand to Noel. "Hey, man," he says. "I'm Jed. Didn't mean to freak you guys out. This place isn't much for streetlights, huh?"

Noel shakes Jed's hand quickly before stuffing his

fists in his pockets. "Guess not," he says. "Lily, I'll, uh . . . I'll call you later?"

I look from Noel to Jed uncertainly. "Sure," I say. Noel lingers, and I lean over to give him a quick peck on the cheek. It feels forced and stupid, and I wish I hadn't done it, but my thoughts are still scrambled and I'm feeling suddenly faint.

"Seems nice," Jed says, watching as Noel reverses down the driveway, his headlights fading away.

"He is." The rain is coming down harder now, the sweatshirt I borrowed from Noel earlier getting damp and heavy.

Jed gestures toward the house. "Is it okay if I come in?"

I stare at the screen door a long moment, as if it might be able to give me advice. It takes a lot to leave me speechless, but I'm having a hard time understanding what I'm supposed to do next. It's almost as if Jed and the island have existed in two entirely different physical dimensions. It feels impossible that they've suddenly collided in the cottage's front yard.

"Lily?" he asks, reaching out to touch my arm. It sends a programmed shock down my spine.

I pull my arm away. "Of course," I say, my voice formal and overly chipper, before starting up the porch stairs. "Come in." Tess and Sammy are at Maya's for dinner, so for better or for worse, we'll have the place to ourselves.

Jed follows me, ducking inside the small front door. His tall frame dwarfs the furniture as though he's stumbled into a miniature diorama. "Cute house," he says, glancing up the stairs and into the living room. I have the urge to stand in front of him, to block his view, to protect this place from his prying eyes.

I take a steadying breath and walk into the kitchen. "Would you like some tea?" I ask, sounding very much like a middle-aged housewife.

Jed sits carefully at the edge of the worn upholstered couch in the living room. "Yeah, or coffee," he answers. I sigh, standing in front of the coffeemaker, annoyed by the prospect of having to brew a whole pot. "Actually, tea's great," he calls out, as if reading my mind.

I fill the kettle with water and catch a glimpse of my reflection in the window over the sink. My hair is wet and flat and my mascara has run into dark pools at the corners of my eyes. I wipe them with the side of one finger and attempt to arrange my hair into something flattering. I silently reprimand myself for caring so much about my appearance, but I know that it's no use. No matter what's happened between us, I'm still that eager-to-please, nerdy little girl, awestruck that Jed Monroe is casually sitting in the other room.

I pull down two mugs and wait for the water to boil, my mind racing with questions. *What is he doing here? Why now? How did he even find me?*

My phone buzzes—Noel. I consider ducking out onto the porch, telling him everything is all right. But I can already hear the strain in my voice, the unconvincing tremble. I decline the call and leave my phone on the counter.

"Thanks," Jed says as I join him in the living room. I place the mugs on a pair of matching tile coasters and sit across from him in one of the high-backed antique chairs, my posture straight and rigid. I clutch the mug with two hands but it burns my palms. I stare at the foggy wisps of steam.

"Terry told me how to find you," Jed says finally. "Don't be mad. I didn't give him much of a choice."

I smile tightly. "There's always a choice."

Jed shrugs. "I gave him my Yankees seats. Behind home plate. Plus, he likes me."

Unfortunately, he's right. In fact, I was surprised that Terry didn't put up more of a fight when we broke up. He was always saying how well Jed and I complimented each other. High praise coming from somebody who could find fault with Mother Teresa if he thought she looked at him funny.

"After I pled my case, I think he felt like you should at least hear me out."

"Your case?"

Jed clears his throat. "I made a mistake," he says. "More than a mistake. I was an idiot. If I could take back the last few months, if I could go back to the way things were . . . you made me happier than I've ever been in my life, Lily. We were good together. Weren't we?"

I lean back in the stiff chair. It's like he's reading from a script I wrote for him in the days and weeks after we first broke up. It's exactly what I dreamed he would say. But now, the words sound different and almost hollow, like the meaning behind them has gotten lost. "I used to think so," I say.

Jed runs one hand through his thick dark hair, droplets of rain landing on his shoulders. "I got scared. One of the guys showed me some dumb article online that said we were getting engaged. That weekend you wanted me to come home to meet your parents? It said I was going to ask your dad's permission to propose. I know it's stupid. I should have just ignored it. But I panicked."

I stare at the faded Oriental rug, the ornate pattern warped through the thick glass of the coffee table. "The weekend of my grandparents' anniversary party?" I ask, working it all out in my head. It was true, what I'd read in the tabloids. He'd lied about not being able to come. But it wasn't because he didn't want to be there. He'd heard a rumor, and he'd been scared that it was true.

"I'm sorry," he says. "It's just . . . it's a lot of pressure. You have to know that."

"Pressure?" I ask. My face is warm and I feel a rising in my chest, like all the things I've been wanting to say to him, to ask him, are pushing up through my ribs. "Pressure to do what?"

As far as I knew, our relationship had been exactly what we both wanted. We worked hard, and what little downtime we had, we spent it together doing low-key, normal things. There was no drama. There were hardly any fights. I can understand feeling freaked out by a rumor online, but at the end of the day, was it worth throwing away everything we had without so much as a conversation about it? "I *never* asked you to do anything you didn't want to do." I can feel righteous anger starting to spread inside me.

"I know." Jed shifts uncomfortably. "It wasn't you. It was . . . everyone else. Everyone on the planet is rooting for you, Lily. They want you to have this perfect love story. A surprise proposal, the perfect ring, a storybook wedding. Do you have any idea what it feels like to be single-handedly responsible for Lily Ross's fairy-tale ending?"

Jed's eyes search mine. I suddenly see the guy I first fell for, the guy on the balcony doing his own thing, refusing to be like everyone else. Of all the people who could have been put in this position, it feels suddenly unfair that it was Jed. Jed, who hates public appearances as much as I love them. Jed, who spends weeks holed up in the studio, obsessing over every last detail of his music. No wonder he was feeling overwhelmed.

"I wish you'd said something," I say, softening.

Jed shakes his head. "I didn't know what to say. It wasn't anything you were doing. There was no way for you to fix it. It's just the way things are." He shrugs.

I stare at him. "If you hate it so much, why did you talk to the press?" I ask. "I saw the magazines. You made me look pathetic."

Jed looks at me squarely in the eyes. "Lily, I didn't say a word," he swears. "It had to have been somebody on my staff, someone who knows my schedule. It wasn't me. You know how I feel about my privacy. I would never have done something like that."

There's something so solid in his voice that it's hard not to believe him.

"Okay," I say. "But what's changed? What's different now? Not my fans. Not my life. As soon as I leave here and get back on the road, everything will be just the same as it's always been. I'm not interested in getting married. That's, like . . . it's a dream, and I want it someday, for sure. But not today. Not tomorrow."

Jed takes a deep breath and I can see the relief flooding him like a current.

"That doesn't mean people are going to stop talking about it," I continue. "I could say I'm not interested in marriage, or a ring, until I'm blue in the face. But the magazines, the blogs . . . they aren't going anywhere."

"I know that," Jed says, "and I'm not saying I have it all figured out. I'm not saying I'm ready to . . . I can't promise I'm ready to be your Prince Charming, if you'd even have me." He clasps and unclasps his long fingers in his lap, looking shyly at the floor, before glancing up at me with a smile. "But I would like the chance to keep auditioning."

My shoulders relax as I fall back into the chair. Rain pounds on the window behind Jed and I still can't believe he's sitting here. Weeks ago, I would have given anything for a big romantic gesture like this one. I may not be twiddling my thumbs, waiting around for a proposal, but my fans are right about one thing: I am a sucker for a happy ending.

Still, now that I'm here on the island, away from the insanity of my everyday life, I'm not even sure what that happy ending looks like. Is it me and Jed, making our music and being together, running around from one event to the next, caught in the machines of our brands, our lives? I can see it, as clearly and easily as ever. Our lives together still make sense. Our relationship is built on the solid ground of our careers, and when our careers are everything, what else matters?

Besides, I can't help but muse guiltily, it would mean I could keep my old album. Maybe *Forever* could be *Forever*, again.

But the memory of Noel's face as he left in the rain, the idea of him sitting at home, wondering if this is it, if everything we were building could be snatched up in an instant, after one visit from that other, bigger life . . . there's a sharp twinge near my heart. I can't look Jed in the eye anymore. I stare into my tea, breathing in the hot steam.

"I don't need an answer right away," Jed says. "Take all the time you need."

I study my hands, my mind, my heart still caught between two places.

"But I was hoping you'd spend the day with me tomorrow."

I look up quickly. "Tomorrow?"

Jed nods. "I have a couple of days off," he says. "I booked a room in town for the night and was hoping you'd show me around. The weather's supposed to clear up. We could go to the beach. Hang out. I don't care. I just . . . I want to be with you," he says, laying one hand on my knee. "I've missed you, Lily. A lot."

I swallow hard and look through the window again at his rental car, imagining him driving it back to the mainland, boarding a plane back to the city. It's a long trip, and it would be a shame for him not to see the island at all. In the beginning, I imagined him everywhere we went, the two of us playing in the waves, cozying up with a blanket at sunset. The picture has faded, but now that he's here, I can start to see flashes of it again. It's easy to move on, to imagine a different future when he's far away and Noel is so close. But now that Jed is here, right here, I feel pulled to give him another chance.

"Just one day," Jed promises. "Then I'll let you get back to work. Terry says you're doing some incredible things out here."

I stare at his hand on my knee, my skin warming beneath the weight of it. It feels strange and familiar at the same time, like a part of me is still stuck in the past, before everything changed, and a part of me is already different. I'm not sure it's possible to go back, but I'm also not ready to give up. Not yet.

"Okay," I agree at last. "One day. That's it."

22

"YOU'D THINK THESE things would come in different sizes."

Jed stands barefoot in the shallow cove, his jeans rolled halfway up his shins, a red kayak bobbing in the water beside him. I'm already nestled into mine, a paddle wedged against the rocky bottom, attempting to push away from shore.

"Coming?" I call over my shoulder. Jed jams his long legs awkwardly into his boat, his knees angled high in front of his face.

Renting kayaks was my idea, and I'd be lying if I said it wasn't meant to be a challenge. Jed has never been much of an outdoorsman; the one time we went hiking near his house in LA, he got spooked by a fallen branch masquerading as a snake. He rarely travels out of his comfort zone, so I'm eager to see how far he'll go, and how serious he is about wanting me back.

"You sure you don't want to get lunch first?" Jed asks, struggling to steer the kayak in a straight line.

"We just had breakfast," I remind him, eyeing the backpack he insisted on bringing from the car. "And you never go anywhere without snacks. Any other excuses?"

Jed lifts his paddle and nudges it against the back of my boat, sending me lurching sideways. "Careful," he teases. "I'm not great with these things."

"You're a quick study," I say, taking short strokes and picking up speed. "Last one there has to tow the other in."

When we reach the point, a quiet, protected stretch of beach, we lug our boats up on the sand. Jed takes a sheet from his backpack and spreads it out near the water's edge. I slip out of my shirt and adjust my bikini top, feeling surprisingly self-conscious. It hadn't taken me long to stop thinking of Jed as *Jed Monroe, Heartthrob*, when we started dating, but now it feels like we're back to square one.

"I could get used to this," he says, stretching out his legs and lying down beside me.

"I already have."

Jed turns to look at me, one hand shielding his eyes from the sun. He studies me carefully. "Fresh air agrees with you, huh?"

I prop myself up on my elbows and look out over the shifting blanket of ocean, the pale blue sky. It feels like we are perched at the end of the world. "The quiet helps me think."

Jed scoops up a handful of sand and sifts a collection of smooth stones through his fingers. "You don't miss the city at all?"

I shrug. "I did at first," I say. "It was hard to get used to having so much free time."

"I bet." Jed leans back on the sheet, rolling up the sleeves of his crisp T-shirt. The pale skin of his upper arms glows in the sun. "Well, the city misses you. Fourth of July just wasn't the same."

He pulls out his phone and holds it up for me to see, swiping through photos of his friends on a glittering rooftop, his friends who became my friends, people I haven't talked to since the breakup. It's funny how seamlessly our lives fit together from the beginning, and then how easy it was for me to slip back out.

I dig my toes into the cool sand, glimpses of red nail polish wiggling through a layer of gray and white pebbles. Jed's right: it wasn't the same for me, either. It wasn't the same at all. I remember the parade, the fireworks, and night swimming with Noel, and I struggle to hide a smile.

"Looks like fun," I say amicably. "But I needed this. I was feeling . . . stuck."

"I know," Jed says. "I can't wait to hear the new stuff. You have anything I can listen to?"

For the past year Jed has been the first to listen to every new song I've written. He's an incredibly skilled musician—more knowledgeable about music theory and songwriting than anyone I've ever met—and I've always valued his opinion. But there's something about the new album that I'm not ready to share with him. It came from a new part of me, a quieter part, a part I'm not sure I want Jed to be critiquing . . . at least not until the whole album is finished.

"Sorry," I lie. "I haven't uploaded anything yet."

Jed smiles. "Maybe later." He sits up and reaches for his backpack, rummaging through the big pocket and pulling out preportioned bags of dried mango and trail mix.

"Squirrel food?" I tease him, dragging the bag toward me and opening the pocket wider. Jed's trainer does his best to combat his carb binges by suggesting healthy snacks. "You don't have anything better in here?"

As I rummage around in the bag my hands land on a thick, oversize envelope. "What's this?" I ask, slipping it from the outside pocket. It's glossy, blue and white with an image of a wave on one side.

Jed looks flustered for a moment. "Open it," he says, smiling timidly. "It's for you."

I peel the top flap open to find two airplane tickets. Not computer printouts, but actual tickets, slipped into one side of the cardboard folder. I read the boxy type on the top line. "Bali?"

"I booked us two weeks at some new eco resort," he says. "Siggy and Lex just got back. They said it was ridiculous. Surfing, great food, all-night parties on the beach . . ."

"You're going to surf?" I ask him incredulously. Given how hard it was to wrangle him into a kayak, it doesn't seem a likely scenario.

"If you want me to." He shrugs, looking out at the ocean. "I think you're on to something, here. Getting away. But I want us to do it together. Things are going to get crazy again when you leave for tour. If we're really going to make this work, we need to get back to where we used to be. Before everything got so . . . messed up."

I stare at the tickets in my hands, the paper trembling slightly between my fingers. In all of the time we've been together, Jed has never talked so openly about our future. I can't believe how much this time apart seems to have affected him. It's like he has magically turned into exactly the person I've always dreamed of being with: full of surprises, planning adventures for us, and totally committed to being together.

"This is . . . incredible," I say quietly, the printed words on the tickets starting to blur in my vision.

I feel Jed inching closer to me on the sheet. "No," he says, taking the tickets in his hand and tapping them gently against my leg. "This is easy."

In the distance, a pair of gulls flies over the ocean, the steady rhythm of their wings perfectly in sync as they flap toward the horizon. He's right. Falling back into our familiar routine, traveling, working . . . it would all be so easy.

But is easy always the answer?

"Hello?"

There's a light on in the kitchen cottage but Sam and Tess had plans to go out with Maya again. The headlights of Jed's departing car swipe across the ceiling and I wish for a minute that I wasn't alone.

"Just me." Noel steps into the doorway, hands in the pockets of his gray fleece vest. "Tess let me in on her way out."

I hear the faraway crunch of Jed's tires on the driveway and wonder how much Noel saw of our good-bye. After a day on the beach Jed suggested dinner in town, but I said I was tired, and promised I'd meet him at the boat tomorrow. I told him I needed time to think, that I'd give him an answer about Bali in the morning. My stomach twists into complicated knots thinking about how much harder it will be to keep a clear head with Noel around.

"I've been texting," Noel says. He's still wearing his fishing boots, faded jeans with soft white patches tucked into the wide rubber tops.

I drop my bag and join him in the kitchen. Lunch dishes still crowd the sink. I pull out one of the mismatched dining chairs for Noel and collapse into the other. He doesn't sit.

"I'm sorry," I say. "I should have called."

"Did you have a nice day?" Noel is having trouble meeting my eye, his gaze trained on the yellow linoleum floor, but I can tell he's genuinely curious. Even when he's upset, even when I've gone MIA and spent the last twenty-four hours with my ex-boyfriend, Noel still wants to know how my day was.

"It was . . . fine. Confusing." My jaw feels tight and tense.

"He wants you back?" Noel asks. He crosses his arms and leans against the wall, then laughs suddenly. "Obviously he wants you back, why else would he come all the way out here, right?"

I manage a sad smile. "I guess so."

Noel nods for a moment, before sitting down in the empty chair across from me. "Look," he says. "I've been thinking. And I know, I know the nice-guy thing to do here would be to tell you that I understand, that whatever you and . . . Jed Monroe had, I'm sure there are things you need to work out, and I should be the bigger person and give you the space to do that."

"Noel, I—" I reach out for his hand.

"Wait." Noel clutches the table tightly between his sturdy fingers. "Let me finish. I've thought about it a lot and this is real, whatever this is between us."

He scratches the back of his head and looks up at the ceiling. I can see the struggle in his whole body, the challenge of getting the right words out, of saying what he means. Of putting himself on the line.

"This is insane." He grimaces. "It's Jed Monroe. The first time I'm ever going to fight for anything, and I'm up against *Jed Monroe*?"

My stomach lurches. I want to tell him that it's not a fight, he's not up against anyone, but I know he won't believe it.

Noel looks at me for the first time, his blue eyes jumpy and unsettled. He holds my hands and takes a breath. "I'm sorry if this makes things harder," he says, "or maybe it doesn't. Maybe you've already decided.

Either way, I had to come here and tell you . . . the last few years have been not so great. Since I came back, I guess I've been sort of stuck. And I wanted you to know that this summer has been . . . it's made me into the best version of myself. The person I wasn't sure I still knew how to be."

I study the rough lines on his hands with my fingers and remember the day we met six weeks ago, the tangle of our cars smoking between us. He'd seemed so confident, so complete, but maybe it was a defense. Maybe he needed just as much help as I did. Maybe the walls I've been so busy tearing down since I got here haven't just been my own.

"I still don't know what this is, and I'm not sure where it's going," he says, "but I'm tired of giving up. I'm not going anywhere, until you tell me to."

There's a threatening lump in my throat and I swallow around it.

"The other day, when we were jumping at the quarry, I wasn't completely honest," he says, curling one hand against the side of my neck. There's a light in his eyes again, something open and full of hope. "I'm not falling for you, Lily Ross. I'm in love with you."

My breath catches in the back of my throat and my pulse whooshes loudly in my ears. Every cell in my body knows it instantly: I love him, too. I love him in a way I haven't loved anyone, or anything, since I was a little girl. I love him like I loved the smell of camp, or singing in the shower, or curling up on the couch with a bowl of buttered popcorn to binge-watch bad movies on a Saturday night. I love him in the same way I love everything about this island. In a way that feels essential.

But is that all it takes? When my life is my music, when so many people are depending on me, waiting for me, rooting for me . . . is loving somebody enough? And as much as it makes me queasy to admit it, even just to myself, there's a part of me that still loves Jed, too. I love the way he knows what he wants and doesn't apologize for being who he is. I love our life together, how seamless and complementary it can be. He messed up, and he hurt me, but am I ready to close that door forever?

My eyes meet Noel's, and my whole body aches. I know he wants to hear that I love him, too, and I want so badly to be able to say it. But the words are stuck in my throat.

"I just need a little time," I finally manage. "Is that okay?"

Noel leans over and tucks a loose strand of my hair back over my shoulder. "Okay," he says, leaning down to sweetly kiss my cheek. Before he pulls away, he whispers into my ear, "Just don't forget to keep jumping."

23

46 Days Until Tour
July 28th

"FEEL YOUR FEET, firmly centered and rooted to the earth."

Tess, Sammy, and I stand in mountain pose on the back deck while Maya faces us, her back to the ocean, her long, thick braid tucked in front of one shoulder. I squeeze my eyes shut but they flicker back open, my body restless and jittery.

"You should feel balanced and at peace."

I snort, louder than I mean to, and Tess nudges me sharply in the back.

"Sorry," I say, my hands flopping out of prayer position. "But I have never been less balanced or at peace in my life."

Maya's eyes flutter open. "Maybe we should do this later?"

I smile at her gratefully but Tess huffs. "No," she says. "If Bird wants to keep agonizing over her Great Summer of Indecision, she can do it alone. We are doing yoga."

Sammy shoots me an apologetic shrug and I sulk away to the porch swing. Tess's words are harsh, but not undeserved. I've spent all morning chasing my friends around the house, rehashing everything that's happened in the last two days: dinner with Noel's family, Jed's surprise appearance, our morning together, the tickets to Bali, Noel's visit last night. They listened patiently as I went back and forth for hours, wondering if I should stay on the island or leave with Jed, hemming and hawing over whether I should give him another chance.

They listened, they asked questions, but they refused to give advice. As I weighed the pros and cons, filled Maya in on the backstory, and struggled to untangle my feelings, I could tell by their silence that they weren't thrilled to watch me stumble my way through yet another romantic mini drama. When Maya suggested yoga after breakfast, we all agreed that I needed a distraction, but I now realize it's going to take more than sun salutations and mindful breathing to help me make up my mind.

"I'm going for a walk," I tell the three of them as they folded into down dog. Sammy lifts one hand to wave, careful not to lose her balance, and Maya offers me an upside-down smile.

I follow the path toward the water and sit at the edge of the long wooden staircase, then close my eyes and listen to the steady rushing of the waves. I have always prided myself on my ability to make decisions quickly, definitively. It's a matter of survival, really; when there are seven hundred decisions to make every day, I usually don't have the time or the energy to think for too long about a single one.

But here, I have all the time in the world. I almost wish there were more distractions, more of a context— however fast-paced and frenzied it may be—to push me in one direction or another.

There are three weeks left until I start rehearsals in New York for the tour. I had planned on spending them here, with my friends. With Noel. I don't feel at all ready to leave yet. Things with Noel have just started to feel real. I'm not sure what will happen when I leave—it hurts too much to think about—but I can't imagine cutting our time together even shorter to fly across the globe to be with somebody else.

But Jed isn't *somebody else*. And he's said all the right things. He isn't asking for a decision; he's asking for a chance, a chance to see if what we had is still there. If we really are supposed to have our version of *happily ever after*, after all.

I drop my head into my hands and tug at the roots of my hair. When it comes to schedules and events, decisions about my brand, even my music, I know what I want without question. But when it comes to love, it's like I'm still that gawky, goofy freshman girl, waiting to screw things up, wishing somebody else would just tell me what to do and how to do it.

"It can't be that bad."

I lift my head to see Maya standing behind me on the path. She holds two glasses of iced tea and passes one to me. "I thought all this communing with nature might be making you thirsty."

I take the glass, beads of condensation dampening my palm, and scoot toward the railing. "Want to sit?" I ask.

Maya settles beside me and stares out at the ocean. There's something about her—maybe it's her steady breathing, or the slow, deliberate way that she moves— that makes her comforting to be around. I can see why Tess likes her so much.

"This is my favorite time of day," she says after a while. "Just before the sun gets really hot. It's like there's an energy everywhere. You can feel things changing, but nothing's happened yet."

I look at the shifting grasses of the marsh, the rustling shrubs, the tidal pools shimmering in the brightening sun. She's right. All around us, the world is tuning up, a giant orchestra waiting for the leading drop of an unseen conductor's baton.

"It must be nice to know a place so well," I say.

"It is," Maya says. "I've traveled a lot, lived in a bunch of different places, but I've never found one that seemed to speak my language the way that this one does. I know that probably sounds hippie-dippie . . ."

I laugh. "Totally hippie-dippie."

Maya smiles and we look out at the endless ocean together, a comfortable quiet hovering between us.

"Did you always know you wanted to stay on the island?" I ask.

"No," she says. "I'm still figuring it out. That's one of the things I like best about this place. Nothing happens in the winter, so pretty much everyone gets away, at least for a little while. It's a good balance. You put yourself out there, you see what's going on, and then you come back to check in. It's sort of like breathing. You get used to the rhythm of taking off and coming home."

"I don't know," I say, turning the cool glass around in my hands. "I do a lot of taking off. I don't think I'll ever get used to it."

Maya looks at me. Her eyes are a soft amber color. "Maybe it's the coming home part you need to work on," she says. "Whatever that means for you."

"I wish I knew." I sigh and look down the long

wooden staircase, the rickety beams leaning against the ancient boulders and steep cliffs. A cloud of tiny black insects zips past and Maya shoos them with one hand.

"I don't know what to do," I say softly. "I know it's ridiculous. I came out here to get away from this kind of thing. Bouncing from one relationship to the next. Getting wrapped up in all this drama. And now I'm right back where I started."

"That's not true," she says. "You may not have found all the answers yet, but I think you know more than you're letting on."

"I do?"

Maya looks at me with a warm smile. "You know what to do," she says. "You're just waiting for it to be easier."

I look at her. "When does that happen?"

Maya smiles. She stares at the ice cubes in her glass, before clinking it lightly against mine. "It doesn't."

Jed's sedan is parked at the end of a short line of cars at the harbor, waiting to get off the island. I rap gently on the darkened window and pull the door open, climbing into the seat beside him.

"Hey," he says, stashing his phone in the center console and turning down the volume on the radio.

"I was starting to think you weren't going to show." I stare through the windshield as the ferry pushes into the harbor, both decks crammed with squinting day-trippers; luggage carts; eager, panting dogs. "Where are your bags?"

I stare at my hands in my lap. "I'm sorry," I say softly.

"You're not coming," he says, almost a question, like he's halfway convinced it's a joke.

I take a long, deep breath. "I can't. It doesn't feel right."

"What does that mean?" he asks coolly. Jed has limited patience for what he calls *touchy-feely talk*. Like me, he's been trained to act quickly and decisively. He makes a plan; he sticks to it. It's not that he intentionally doesn't follow his heart; he just doesn't spend a lot of time consulting it.

"It means that I've worked really hard to get here," I say patiently.

"Where?" He looks around dramatically at the parking lot, the minivans overloaded with beach gear, the work trucks jammed with fishing poles and tools. "Here?"

I squeeze the sides of my bare knees between my hands, the fraying ends of my cutoffs tickling my wrists. "I was feeling stuck, like I was writing the same songs over and over again. And now I'm not. I have to honor that. I have to believe that I'm here for a reason."

"Is this about that guy?" It's the first time Jed's mentioned Noel since they met in the driveway. I thought for sure he'd want to know more about him, but he hasn't even asked his name. "The guy from the other night?"

I shift uncomfortably on the leather seat. "He's part of it," I admit. "But it's more than that. I like who I am here. I haven't felt this way about a place since I was a kid."

Jed raises an eyebrow at me. "What about who you are everywhere else? What's going to happen when you go back on tour?" he asks. "He's going to come with you?"

"I don't know," I say softly. "Maybe it's time for me to put down some roots and . . . I don't know, take a real break."

"A break?" Jed asks. "You mean, from touring?"

"Maybe," I say. "Every relationship I've been in has ended because of my career, or somebody else's. Everything I've done, every thought that's come into my head has had something to do with work. It's been nice to turn that off. If I can't be happy and make music at the same time, what's the point?"

Jed looks at me like I've suddenly sprouted extra body parts. "The point?" He reaches across the car and puts a hand on my shoulder, like I'm falling and he's trying to hold me up. He leans in so that I have no choice but to look at him. "The point is you don't get to choose, Lily.

Your voice, your songs . . . that's who you are. You can hole up at the end of the earth for as long as you want, but you're still going to have this gift. If you can't find a way to live with that *and* someone else, I don't care who it is . . . you're never going to be happy."

24

IT'S LATE WHEN K2 drops me off and I half expect/ half hope to find Noel's shack empty. But one window is lit up by the lamp on his desk, and I can see his hunched-over silhouette through the old blue-and-white-striped sheet he's rigged up as a curtain.

Since Jed left this afternoon, I haven't been able to get his words out of my head. *You're never going to be happy.* What if he's right? No matter how much I try to make things work with Noel, no matter how much I love being here on this island, could I ever truly be happy without making my music, seeing my fans, singing my songs on tour? I can't just pretend that's not a part of me anymore. The songs I've written since I've been here . . . I'm prouder of them than I am of anything else I've done. It wouldn't feel right not to share them just because I've decided to be *happy*. And what about the songs I write next? Even if staying here with Noel is what my heart wants most, it doesn't mean I can—or should—do it.

But I don't want to leave him. The idea of moving on without him hits me like a swift kick to the stomach. When I think about losing him, I can't breathe.

I knock twice on the door before pushing it open. "Noel?" Moths swarm the naked lightbulb that hangs over the patio and I shut the door again before they flutter in behind me.

Noel is at his desk in plaid flannel pants and a T-shirt. His hair is wet and tousled and a towel is in a damp heap on the dusty wood floor. "Hey," he greets me, startled. He shoves his chair back, and steps forward like he wants to hug me, but then stops awkwardly, as if he isn't sure if it's still allowed. Instead, he tucks his hands in his pockets, biting the inside of his cheek.

I've never been in his little house before. The space is crowded, with hardly any room between each piece of mismatched furniture: the square kitchen table that doubles as a desk, a squat chest of drawers, the lofted bed pushed against the windowless back wall.

He looks around uncertainly. "Sorry. There isn't really any place to sit. I mean, there's the chair, but it's not really comfortable. It used to have a cushion but it smelled like moldy cheese, so I took it to the dump," he explains, the sides of his neck flushing pink. "I don't know why I just told you that."

I laugh and take a step forward, so that it's almost impossible for our bodies not to touch. I put my hands on his shoulders and kiss him. I feel his arms folding around my back, pulling me in closer. We stay like that for what feels like an eternity, balanced against each other. I feel my body going slack, like it could melt into his. I don't ever want to pull away.

Noel leans back ever so slightly, our noses still centimeters apart. "Does this mean you've made up your mind?"

I run my hands down the smooth contours of his strong arms and quickly kiss him again. "It means that I'm jumping," I say. "I love you, too, Noel Bradley."

Noel links his arms around my waist and pulls me tightly to him. His grip is so strong that my feet leave the ground. When he puts me back down, I rest my head on his shoulder. Something on his desk catches my eye: an open notepad beside a pile of stubby charcoal pencils. There's a half-finished sketch of a boat—his boat, shadowed and full of breathtaking detail.

"Did you do this?" I ask, leaning in to get a closer look.

"What?" Noel asks. "Oh. Yeah. I needed something

to take my mind off . . . everything," he explains shyly.

"It's incredible," I say. "You drew this on your own? I mean, it's not from a picture?"

Noel smiles and taps the side of his head. "Just what's in here. I've probably spent more time on that boat than anywhere else on the planet," he says with a shrug. "I know it pretty well."

I flip through the notebook and find a series of equally impressive drawings—a tower of rusty lobster crates, a surfboard angled against a tree—each one more precise than the last.

Eventually, I look up from the drawings, at him, ideas suddenly flooding my brain. "Come with me," I say all at once, like it's the only option.

"What?" Noel laughs lightly, closing the notebook and stuffing the pencils inside an old mason jar. "Come with you where?"

"Everywhere," I say. "I don't want to leave you. And I don't want to leave the island. But I have to go. I'll always have to go. Touring is . . . it's why I do this. At least for now . . . being onstage, seeing my fans, it's everything to me."

Noel sinks down onto the chair, a conflicted look passing over his face. I reach out and grab one of his hands. "It's *almost* everything," I say. "What we have is so amazing. And I don't want it to end when the summer does. I want you there with me. It will be totally nuts—weeks of rehearsals, living out of suitcases, flying every other night—but I'll have some days off, and it will just feel . . . right, knowing that you're always nearby."

Noel blinks slowly, like he's suddenly exhausted. I curl into his lap, looping my arm around his neck. "And when we're not together, you can do this." I nod at the notebook on the table. "Or whatever you want! I know how much you love it here—and I love it, too—but the island isn't going anywhere. Come with me."

I feel myself starting to slip down his legs and Noel hauls me closer. He glances out through the window, toward the main house, where the pale blue flicker of the television glows from the living room.

"I don't know," he says softly. "I don't know if I can leave them."

My eyes float up to Sidney's bedroom window. I imagine her wedged between two computers, hard at work beneath a web of thumbtacks and postcards, dreaming of who she'll someday be.

"I know," I say, tucking an errant strand of silky hair behind Noel's ear. "But promise me you'll think about it."

Noel nods vaguely and I lean in to give him another kiss. "And I promise not to distract you," I say between fluttery kisses. "Too much."

25

"THIS THING IS a total beast."

Sidney squats in the front yard, a rusty lawn mower turned on its side in the dry grass beside her. Her hands and jeans are covered in grease, and there's a black smudge near her ear, where she uses one forearm to wipe her frizzy blond hair away from her face.

"What are you doing?" I ask, pushing through the screen door of Noel's shack. It's been over a week since Jed left, and I've spent nearly all of it at Noel's house, hanging with Sid and their dad, or out on the boat. I called Terry a few days ago, and we're going forward with the plan for a tour tie-in EP. "Anchors" will be out as a single by the last week of rehearsals, which should be enough time to get people excited. With the anxiety of finishing the music off my chest, I've been able to relax—I want to enjoy the rest of my time here, since the future with Noel is still an unknown. We haven't talked much about what comes next, but the question is always there, like a secret, a hidden, special electricity constantly flickering back and forth between us.

"Dad said if I take this thing apart and figure out what's wrong with it, he'll buy the parts I need to fix it," Sidney says, wrestling the metal innards apart with scary-sounding clanks and groans.

"And then you get to use it!" Noel calls out from behind the wooden doors of the outdoor shower, where he's busy fiddling with a leaky pipe.

"No dice," Sid mutters in response. "I don't mow. I tinker."

I pull up an old lawn chair. A few of the rubber slats are twisted and broken but I manage to get comfortable, crossing my ankles in the grass. I peer into the mess of gears and wires, watching Sidney work. With her low, furrowed brow and set jaw, she looks just like Noel does when he's on the boat, working.

"You like this stuff, huh?" I ask.

Sidney grunts and sifts through a pile of tools. "Beats working on my tan." She rolls her eyes. "That's what the girls in my class do all summer long."

"You don't like the beach?"

"Who said anything about the beach?" she scoffs. "They all meet up at Laura McMahon's house, the big one at the end of the point? She's got this huge deck and they line up their towels and fry like skinny pink sausages."

The shower whines and squeals as Noel turns it on and off to test it, and I hear him chuckling.

"They do!" Sid insists. "I can't wait to get out of this place."

I pull my sunglasses out of my hair and settle them onto my face. "Where you headed?"

"Anywhere but here," she says, twisting a wrench deep inside the tangled machinery. "Gonna meet up with Mom somewhere as soon as I graduate. Maybe go to college if I get in."

"If you get in?" Noel pops out from behind the shower door, drying his hands on his striped board shorts. "You've been taking community college classes since the seventh grade. You can go anywhere you want."

Sidney grunts again, struggling to disconnect two pieces of twisted metal. There's a faraway look in her eyes, like her body is here but the rest of her is somewhere else. Her focus is mesmerizing.

"Who wants ice cream?" Noel asks, ducking into the cottage to switch out his dirty shirt for a clean white one. "My treat."

I hop up from the chair and stretch my arms high over my head, tilting my face to the sun. "I do."

"Sid? You coming?" Noel asks.

She ignores us for a few seconds before tossing the wrench at the ground. "Fine," she says. "I need to read the manual anyway. Hopefully it's in Japanese. I'm working on my translation." Sid walks briskly toward the house.

"Ask Dad if he wants anything," Noel calls after her.

Sid waves him off. "Real ice cream. Not frozen yogurt," she demands, before disappearing into the house.

I laugh as Noel grabs my hand and leads me to the truck. He sits on the hood and I snuggle between his legs, my back against the bumper.

"You're getting freckles," he says, looking down and playfully tapping my nose.

I swat his hand away. "I know," I say. "I'll never hear the end of it."

"I like it," Noel says, squeezing me around the waist. "If that counts for anything."

"It does," I say, tilting my face up to give him a kiss.

"So where to first?" Noel asks, settling back against the windshield. I hop up on the hood beside him.

"Ice cream," I answer. "Right?"

Noel reaches for my hand. "I meant on tour," he says,

staring at our fingers as they tangle together. "It's coming up fast."

"Six days until I leave." A pit opens up in the bottom of my stomach and I start to feel faint. This has been happening lately, whenever I think about leaving, so I've made a concerted effort not to do it.

"But who's counting," Noel teases. "What's the first stop on the tour?"

"LA," I say. "But I have a few weeks of rehearsals in New York first."

"Cool," Noel says. "That should give me some time to learn my way around."

"What?" I shift abruptly on the hood to face him. I pull our hands, still woven together, into my lap. He smiles slyly. "You're coming?" I practically screech.

Noel shrugs. "If you'll have me."

"Yes!" I wrap him in a hug. "I mean, sure, if that's what you want . . ." I clear my throat and feign disinterest, smoothing my features into a mask of nonchalance. Noel laughs and hugs me tight. There's a lightness spreading throughout my body, the hollow in my stomach filling up with warmth.

"What about work?" I ask, pulling away to glance back at the house. "What about Sid? Your dad?"

Noel turns his rope bracelet against the knobs of his sturdy wrist. "They'll be fine," he says. "They've got their own little routine down now. I mostly just get in the way."

I study him carefully, skeptically. "You're sure you won't miss this place?"

"I'll definitely miss it," he says. "But like you said, it's not going anywhere. *You* are."

I put a hand on the soft sleeve of his T-shirt and lean in to kiss him.

"I thought we agreed this was a PDA-free zone," Sidney shouts from the driveway, hurrying toward the truck. "Don't make me separate you two."

Noel holds my hand as we hop down from the truck. "I'd like to see you try."

"Lily, that was spectacular."

I set my guitar on my knees and reach for a glass of water. The booth is hot and sticky, my throat dry and parched. As the countdown to tour continues, Terry has convinced me to schedule a few short interviews and radio spots. I've spent the better part of the afternoon—a perfect, cloud-free beach day—locked in the dark, musty sound booth of the local high school's radio station, whipping through interviews and live performances, while Sammy and Tess make faces from the other side of the glass. I've played "Anchors" at least six times, landed on the same, Terry-approved sound bites ("Time away has been just what I've needed" and "I can't wait to get back on the road and hang out with my fans!"), and only mixed up the superanimated hosts' names twice.

This one, Joey Z out of Tucson, sounds like a chipmunk on speed. He zips through the usual roster of questions about the new album, the breakup, and my self-imposed exile from the city. But then, just as I feel the interview winding down, he catches me off guard:

"So tell us about this Noel guy," he stage-whispers for dramatic effect. "I'm guessing he's the anchor we're hearing so much about? Sure looks like he's got a hold on you, from what I can see."

Sweat prickles under my arms. *What he can see?* There's a rapping on the window and I look up to see that Sammy is holding her phone to the glass. Her browser is pulled up to TMZ, and there on the homepage is a full-page photo of Noel, Sid, and me getting ice cream yesterday in town. Noel and I are holding hands, and Sidney trails behind us, the cone angled to her face, mid-bite.

"Lil-y," Joey Z teasingly intones, "anything you want to tell us?"

I breathe carefully, making sure to turn my face away from the headset before adjusting the microphone. Normally, I don't say anything about my personal life that hasn't been vetted by Terry and the team. And rarely am I caught off guard by photos in the press. If I'm seen in public holding hands with someone new, it's usually because I want to be. I know the "right" thing to do here would be to deny it. Say Noel's just a friend—a family friend, maybe, something innocent and concrete.

But something in me can't find the words, or the practiced, blasé tone I'd need to pull them off. What am I hiding from? Noel isn't like the other guys I've dated. He doesn't have a manager, a publicity machine. On the island, we're just another couple, doing what couples do. Everything is different now. Why shouldn't this be different, too?

"Joey," I say, breathy and casual. "You know I don't kiss and tell. But I will say that he's someone very special to me, and I can't wait for you all to meet him soon."

I see Sammy and Tess cringe as Joey Z hoots and hollers.

"Does this mean he'll be joining you on tour this fall?"

Tess is already on the phone and Sammy is holding her head in her hands. I know I should be terrified, but instead, I feel like I'm floating, like half my heart has been locked in chains and now, suddenly, it's free.

"Nothing's set in stone yet," I say. "But I can say it would make me very happy if he did."

26

35 Days Until Tour
August 8th

SAMMY PUSHES MY phone toward me across the backseat as K2 whips around the island's dirt roads toward the house. "It's Terry."

I try to read her face for some clue as to what I'm in for, but her lips are tight, her eyes a trained mask of indifference. I've forgotten what my friends are like when things get hairy. Being away has changed them, too. They've been more relaxed, less consumed by the minutia of my daily life, and it's almost scary how immediately they've snapped back into work mode. There are subtle differences in the tone they use to talk to me now and in their neutral, studied expressions.

I hold my breath and bring the phone to my ear,

steeled against the barrage of reprimands I suspect are about to be spewed in my direction.

"Hello?" I greet him meekly.

"Lily!" Terry booms. "You were brilliant!"

My eyebrows cinch together. "I was?"

"The stuff about the guy? How you can't wait for us to meet him? Sheer genius!" Terry laughs. "And of course he's a dreamboat. I mean, my God, where do you find these people?"

I chuckle nervously. Terry's acting like this was some publicity play, like coming clean about Noel was a premeditated plan to get more press before the tour. I suddenly start to feel sick.

"I hate to make this about me," he continues, "but can I just remind you that I never fell for that 'the island is my anchor' baloney? Not for one second."

Terry babbles on about ramping up my interviews to stay in control of the way the story plays out. I try to pay attention but my head is spinning. *The story?* Noel isn't a story. He's a person.

My legs start to twitch. I have to get off the phone. I have to call Noel. I stammer some stuff to Terry about a bad connection and hang up as we pull into the driveway.

"Bird—" Tess says from the front seat.

"Hang on," I interrupt, finding Noel's number. "I need to make sure that Noel isn't going to kill me."

K2 cuts the engine and the car is suddenly too quiet. Tess and Sammy are turned to look out their windows. "I'd say he's getting there," Tess says.

Noel's truck is in our driveway, and he stands beside it, his face frozen somewhere between bewilderment and sheer panic.

"You have to get him out of here," Sammy says.

"What do you mean?"

Tess looks over our shoulder. "She's right. Unless you want this conversation broadcast on the nightly news, you need to have it somewhere other than the driveway."

I hear the rumble of wheels on gravel and turn to see a pair of cars squealing to a stop at the end of the road. "Are you kidding me?" I ask as a cluster of camera-wielding paparazzi forms at the edge of the lawn. "How is this happening? Nobody could have gotten here this fast."

"The photos went up early this morning, and apparently the paparazzi showed up on the island soon after," Tess explains. "I guess town has been a circus all day. When the interview went live, they must have found us at the station and followed us here."

Tess flings her door open and starts toward Noel, while Sammy nudges me out of the car. "Go inside," she says. "Don't run. Don't look concerned. Just walk like a normal person."

I force what I hope is a casual smile and glance over at Noel. Tess is putting an arm around him and undoubtedly giving him the same orders, and they walk slowly, if rigidly, toward the house.

"Lily!" I hear the first of the catcalls coming from behind us. The crowd has grown to about six reporters, scrambling to get their shots.

"Wave," Sammy whispers, and I lift a hand, beaming a manufactured smile before following her up the steps.

"Noel, I'm so sorry."

We're alone in the kitchen—Sam and Tess have gone upstairs to man their phones and keep up with what's happening online. Noel leans against the refrigerator and I reach for the ragged hem of his faded gray T-shirt, tugging it gently. He tries to smile, but his eyes are jumpy and uncertain.

"I was . . . I was pulling into the harbor and they were all there, with cameras, and so many questions." He scratches the back of his head. "I just wish I knew what I was supposed to say."

"I know." I nod, looping my arms around his waist. "I'm sorry. I should've . . . we should have talked about it first. I should have warned you about this part. I just, I got caught up, and . . . I'm tired. I'm tired of thinking about everything that I say, or being told how I should spin things. This, us"—I put a hand on his chest—"it doesn't need spinning."

But even as I say the words, I feel guilty. I feel Noel's pulse racing beneath my palm. How could I not have considered what this would be like for him? His whole life will be analyzed, his every move will be held under a spotlight and picked apart for weeks.

I reach for his hand and wish more than anything that I could lead us somewhere safe, where we could be alone, just us. It's the way I used to feel, when I was just starting out and didn't know how to handle how crazy everything would get. Back before I learned how to be "on" all the time. I remember how terrifying it was, how violated I felt that I couldn't walk outside my front door without feeling like it was a performance. All I wanted was to hide beneath my covers, to wake up in a world where nobody knew my name.

Now, without so much as a word of warning, I've done the same thing to Noel.

I force a reassuring smile, trying to calm us both down at the same time. "It's going to be intense for a little while," I finally manage, hoping he doesn't hear it for what it truly is: the understatement of the century.

"Intense?" Noel raises a concerned eyebrow.

I nod. "They'll want to know everything about us,

about you," I say. "But the good news is, it doesn't last long. Once they see how boring we are, they'll be on the next boat out of here, I promise."

Noel laughs, and I can see color returning to his cheeks. "Lily Ross and Boring Local: Netflix and Chill?" he jokes hopefully.

My ragged breathing starts to even out, the tense knots in my shoulders start to unwind. "You heard it here first."

I push myself up onto my toes and nestle against his chest, hoping that he's right. Of course there will be some photos, a story or two, but once the newness wears off, maybe they'll leave us alone. I close my eyes and breathe deeply into his shoulder, inhaling the familiar smell of sea salt and soap.

"Lily?"

I pull my head away to see Tess in the doorway. The look in her eyes is sharp and alarming. Before she says a word, I know: they'll never leave us alone.

Things have gotten much, much worse.

"What is it?" I ask.

She walks slowly toward us with her phone. She hands it to me, but her eyes are glued to Noel.

The screen is open to another gossip blog, one that I've barely heard of, and the homepage has a photo of a woman who looks vaguely familiar, but whom I can't place right away. The longer I look the more I realize that the photo is a mug shot, a grainy, washed-out close-up of a pale, thin woman standing in front of a blank white wall. "Who is this?" I ask, waving the phone back at Tess.

Tess doesn't say anything, her gaze still locked on Noel as he leans in for a look. His face goes slack, his jaw drooping and his eyes growing wide. "It's my mother," he says, slightly above a whisper. "It's my mom."

There's a buzzing sound in my head and I feel an inappropriate laugh bubbling up in my throat. I look frantically from Noel to Tess, who takes back her phone and scrolls down through the story.

"What do you mean, it's your mom?" I ask him, peering over his shoulder to get another look.

My mind flashes back to the black-and-white photo on the wall of his house, his mom, pregnant, with Noel beside her. This woman is older and thinner, with new, hard lines on her face and dark shadows around her eyes. But there's no question: It's the same woman. It's Noel's mom.

I shake my head, as if I'm trying to rearrange pieces of a scattered puzzle. "I don't get it," I say. "I thought she was in India."

Noel slides down the refrigerator, landing on the floor. He bends his knees and draws them close to his body, lowering his head into his hands. I crouch down beside him and put my hands on his shoulders. I wait for him to say something, but he just stares at a spot on the linoleum between my feet.

"Noel?" I urge, looking from him back up at Tess. "What's going on?"

Tess stares at the top of Noel's head, her lips twisted in a knot. Noel makes a groaning sound and I look back into his eyes. There's a sudden harshness to his features that I've never seen before. He looks older. Weaker. He looks just like his father.

"What's going on?" Noel slowly repeats, forcing a hard chuckle behind it. "What's going on is that my mother isn't in India. She's in rehab outside of Portland, where she's been since she was arrested two years ago."

"Arrested?" I ask. The urge to laugh is back. This has to be a joke. *Rehab?* How could I not have known? "What are you talking about?" I ask again. "You said . . ."

"She's an addict, Lily," Noel says, a wounded weariness coating his voice. "She's an alcoholic and an addict, and my dad kicked her out. She got picked up on the mainland with drugs in her car, spent a few nights in jail, and my dad said the only way he'd bail her out was if she got help. She was in rehab for a while and has been living in a halfway house ever since."

Tess puts a hand on Noel's shoulder and for a strange, confusing moment I feel like a third wheel. Something in me even wonders if I should leave them alone. There's no way Tess could have known the truth, but she must remember his mom the way she used to be. They have a past together, a shared history, something I'll never understand. How can I comfort him when there's so much I still don't know about him? How can I help him when it's my fault he's hurting in the first place?

Tess glances at me and puts the phone in her pocket. "I'll be upstairs," she says, giving Noel's shoulder one last squeeze before quietly slipping into the hall.

Noel is gripping the ends of his light hair and blinking furiously at the floor. I sit cross-legged beside him. I close my eyes and see Sidney, the map on her wall, the pushpins, the postcards.

"Sidney . . ." I say, starting to work it all out.

"She doesn't know," Noel finishes, a new flash of panic registering on his face. "She *didn't* know. Fuck."

He scrambles to his feet, bumping a chair and knocking it to the floor with a jarring crash. I cringe and reach out to stop him as he starts for the door.

"She doesn't know what?" I stand.

"Anything!" Noel shouts, flustered. "She thought . . . we've been . . ."

I feel the blood draining from my face. "You've been lying to her?" I guess. "Your dad?"

"It was his idea," Noel blurts, pacing the kitchen with

his arms over his head, like he's been running too long and is walking out a cramp. "This island . . . it's so small. He didn't want her to be *that* kid at school. It would have been all anyone talked about. It's hard enough for her as it is, you know? She's different." He looks at me, his eyes suddenly searching mine, begging me to understand. "We were just trying to protect her."

I bend down slowly to pick up the fallen chair and let my body sink against it. "What about the postcards?" I ask.

"That was Mom's idea," Noel says. "She orders a bunch online and sends them in an envelope to a PO box. My dad picks them up so Sid doesn't see the postmark. Mom says it's the only thing that keeps her going, pretending to be somewhere else."

I feel my eyes watering and wipe at them quickly. "So everyone's in on it but Sid?" I ask. Something bubbles in my chest and I feel like I'm the one who's been betrayed. How could they not tell her the truth? She's smarter than the rest of us put together. Did they honestly think she wouldn't figure it out, eventually? "She's fourteen, Noel," I say, my voice harder now, almost accusatory. "She's not a little kid."

Noel stops moving and whips around to point a finger in my face. "You don't get to judge me. You have no idea what it's like," he says. "You have no idea what *anything's* like. You think this island is a bubble, Lily? You're a bubble. Your whole life . . . it's not even real. You complain about not being able to do what you want? To think for yourself? All you *do* is think about yourself!"

I sit frozen at the table, stung by his words.

"Did you ever stop to think that maybe I didn't want you to write a song about me? That maybe I wouldn't want my entire life picked over by complete strangers?" Noel stares at me, like he's waiting for an answer.

My breath gets quick and shallow; my chest feels like it's collapsing. I see myself again, the way I used to be, before all this became a way of life. Seeing my innermost secrets splashed across the pages of magazines, explaining myself in carefully rehearsed sound bites at every turn . . . only, when it happens to me, there's a flip side. I still get to make my music. I still get to travel around the world. I still get to sing my songs to thousands of people in the dark.

What does Noel get?

I drop my head onto the table. I don't know what else to say. Noel throws up his hands and turns to the doorway, standing with his back to me. I look up to see that Tess and Sammy are hovering in the hall.

Suddenly, awfully, Noel laughs. He gestures to my friends as he walks toward them. "Even your friends have to be paid to hang out with you," he calls back to me, cruelly, over his shoulder. "You don't see a problem with that?"

Tears pool in the corners of my eyes, clouding my vision as I stare at a chipped corner of the kitchen table. I see the shape of Tess's arm as she reaches out for Noel, a quick flurry of color and motion as he brushes her off. I hear the hurried shuffle of his footsteps. I feel the shattering quake of the door as it slams behind him.

27

I SPEND THE next few days in bed. At least, my body does. My mind is somewhere else, everywhere else, cycling through events—the things I've done and said, the things Noel said, the looks on my friends' faces as they stood like statues in the hall—and wondering how it all could have gone so wrong, so fast.

I was happier than I'd ever been. I'd finally done it, finally found a way to have everything I've ever wanted. My music, my fans, my career . . . and a normal, stable relationship with a guy who cared about me as much as I cared about him.

But now I'm back to square one: a life that will never be normal.

I flop my head against the pillow. Every so often, I hear myself making weird noises, low, guttural groans, like I'm being passed through some invisible torture device, my insides twisted into unbearable knots. How could I have been so thoughtless? Going public should have been something that Noel and I decided together. If he'd had all the facts about what he was getting into, maybe he wouldn't have wanted to come on tour with me, but at least he would have been prepared.

I sit up, staring out the dark window. It's night again. Soon, Sammy will bring me something to eat, a simple, lovingly prepared meal that I'll barely be able to pick at. Tess will read through my emails and keep me up-to-date on what's going on at home, how the set for tour is coming along, who's doing what and what's being planned. I'll nod and thank her, blankly, without actually hearing a word that she's said.

My phone buzzes, buried beneath the comforters. I've been ignoring it for days, racking up voice mails and texts alerts in terrorizing little red bubbles. But this time, something tells me to look.

It's my mom.

I swipe the screen and press the phone to my cheek. I try to say "hi" but all that comes out is a pathetic-sounding cry.

"Sweetie?" Mom says. I hear the beeping sound her

car makes when the door is open, the rumble of her engine as it starts. "Honey, what's wrong?"

"I ruined everything," I say once my breath has steadied and I seem to be out of tears. "I forgot what it's like. I forgot how easy it is for me to hurt people I care about, without even thinking."

"Honey, we've been over this," Mom says. Hours after the story about Noel's mother broke, Mom called. I could tell that she wanted to fly out, to be with me, and part of me wanted nothing more than to let her. To have her sit in bed beside me, rub my back and tell me everything was going to be all right. But it felt wrong. *Sidney* is the one who should be able to get a hug from her mom whenever she needs it, whispered reassurances, a cheerleader when times are tough. Not me.

"This isn't your fault," Mom says for the zillionth time. "It's a shame, what happened, but you didn't do this."

I shake my head, as if she can see me from her car. "What if he's right?" I say. "What if I'm not the person I think I am?"

I hear Mom sigh, her blinker clicking in the background. "Do you remember when we used to get the piano tuned? The upright we had in the old house?"

I stare at my teary reflection in the window, rubbing damp circles away from my face. "The motorcycle guy?" I ask. Once a year my parents would have our secondhand piano tuned by a guy who showed up on a Harley, lugging a shoulder bag of tools and instruments and leaving behind a trail of musty cologne.

"Yes," Mom says, and I can hear her smiling. "You used to love him. You'd hang around him like a puppy dog, until I made you sit on the steps to stay out of his way. You watched him plunk the keys and duck his head under the lid for hours. When he was finished, he always played a few bars of the same song—I think it was the Beatles or something—just to make sure it sounded all right."

"'Let It Be,'" I say with a smile, the memory flooding my senses. I can see his leather coat as he sat on the too-small wooden bench, I can hear the tinny chords as they rang out in our cramped living room.

"One year you came to me in the kitchen, practically in tears. You were so upset. Do you remember what you said?"

"I asked you to let him finish," I say.

Mom laughs. "That's right," she says. "As if I had told him he couldn't. So we went in there together and you asked him if he'd play that song for you all the way through. He looked like he was going to cry, like it was all he wanted to do. And he played the song, and you sat there with that sweet smile . . ." Mom trails off. "You know exactly what people want, Lily. It's like a sixth sense. All you've ever tried to do is make people happy. You do it with your music, and you do it by putting yourself out there, again and again. It takes courage to do what you do. Sometimes it can be hard for other people to understand. But it's who you are."

I hear a sniffle on the phone and then a chuckle. "I'd say it's who we raised you to be, but I can't take any credit," she says. "I was just worried that guy was going to sit on my sofa in his greasy motorcycle pants."

I tell Mom that I love her and that I can't wait to see her in a few weeks—she and Dad always come to the first few cities of a tour, to sit front row and help me transition back to life on the road.

I hang up and hear a knock at the door. Sammy and Tess peek in. Sammy sets a plate of food on the bedside table, grilled cheese and tomato soup, my childhood favorite. "Admit it," she says, watching as my eyes light up. "Nine-year-old you is so totally psyched right now."

I laugh and nod. "Totally," I agree. "Thank you."

Tess sits at the end of my bed, her phone loose in her palm. She looks at me apologetically. "Should we get this over with?"

"I guess." I sigh, pulling the plate onto my lap and biting into the sandwich.

"Okay," she says, opening the first email. "So

wardrobe sketches are in, and I think you're going to really . . ."

"Wait," I say suddenly, my mouth half full of hot, melty cheese. I swallow and put the plate back on the table. "Stop. Sorry, I just . . . I want to . . . I have to say something first."

Tess and Sammy look at me expectantly. I smile at them, my best friends, the people who know what I want, who anticipate what I need and bend over backward to give it to me, every time, all the time, without me even asking.

Except that I do ask. I've asked them to be here, to do these things, to put my life before theirs. And they've agreed to do it. It's worked, for a while. But now, I want something else. I don't want them to worry about giving me bad news. I don't want them to plan my days, or cook for me, or manage my correspondence.

I want my best friends back.

I take a deep breath. "You're fired."

Tess and Sammy look quickly at each other.

Tess scoffs. "What are you talking about?"

Sammy glances at the bedside table. "Is this about the grilled cheese?" she asks. "I can make you something else."

I put a hand on her knee. "No," I say. "The grilled cheese is perfect. Everything you guys do, everything you've done, has been perfect. But I can't do this anymore. I asked you to work for me because I couldn't imagine spending so much time with anyone else. And I've loved every minute of having you around. But you can't stop living your lives just because it's easier for me."

Tess shakes her head. "Noel was upset," she says. "What he said, about paying us—"

"He was right," I interject. "You're my best friends. When things go wrong in my life, I want to be able to call you and complain. I want you to tell me that I'm being crazy, that I'm thinking too much, or not enough, or whatever."

"We do that anyway," Sam says, anxious wrinkles creasing her forehead.

"I know you do," I say. "I just don't want you to worry about what I'm doing the other twenty-three hours of the day. You have your own lives to live. It's time for you to start living them."

Sam looks at me, her eyes pooling with tears. I wrap her in a hug. "It's going to be okay," I say. "It's going to be better than okay."

Sam nods uncertainly. "I'm scared," she says, biting her full lower lip.

I nod, squeezing her hand. "Me too," I say. "But we're all still going to be—"

"No." She shakes her head. "It's not that."

Tess looks at her, an eyebrow raised. "Sam?" she asks. "What's up?"

Sammy looks back and forth from Tess to me. "I'm going back to school," she says. "In Madison. I'm going to be a nurse."

"What?" Tess and I exclaim in unison.

"Since when?" Tess follows up.

Sammy pulls at the bunched-up blankets between her crossed legs on my bed. "I've been taking an online class all summer. Biology. It's a prerequisite, and I need to pass before I start up in the fall. It's impossible. I've spent practically every night with these textbooks . . ."

"So *that's* what you've been locked away reading," I say with a smirk.

Sam nods. "Trying, anyway," she says. "I don't think I can do it."

"Of course you can do it," I say. "You work harder than anyone I know."

"I work hard because I have to," Sam huffs. "The only thing I've ever been any good at is this, helping you. At least with you, I know what I'm doing."

Tess rolls her eyes and gives Sammy's shoulder a shove. "Don't be so dramatic," she says. "Of course you can do it. And if it doesn't work out, I'm sure there are a hundred needy pop stars who would love your grilled cheese sandwiches."

I nudge Tess gently and lean in to grab Sammy's hand. "This is so great," I say.

"You think so?" Sam asks.

"I do."

Tess shifts on the bed and I look at her. "What about you?" I ask. "Do you ever think about going back to school?"

"Hell no," Tess answers. "I'm riding these coattails as far as they'll take me, I don't care what you say."

We all laugh, and Tess fidgets with the straps of her tank top. "Kidding," she says. "But I'm not sure what I'll do. Maya wants to go to Brazil . . ." She shrugs casually.

Sammy and I raise our eyebrows at each other, as Tess looks at the floor, little red patches blooming on her cheeks. Tess has rarely spent more than a night at a girlfriend's apartment, let alone followed one to a different continent.

Though I've been too distracted to realize it, both of my friends have spent this summer taking chances, learning about themselves and who they are, without me. It took me a while to figure it out, but we've all ended up at the same place. I'm so proud of them, of all of us, that my heart feels like it could explode.

"Send me a postcard?" I tease Tess, and she nods. Sammy sniffles and we both wipe our eyes.

Tess pushes herself off the bed. "Jesus, enough with the hysterics," she says. "At least you still have a job."

I roll my eyes and flop heavily back into the pillows on my bed. "Do I?"

Tess tosses her phone onto my outstretched legs. "According to the eleven hundred emails you'll now be reading for yourself, I'd say you do, whether you like it or not."

Sammy squeezes my ankle and I hear them start back down the stairs.

I stare up at the ceiling for a few moments, the cool night breeze rustling the curtains. I reach for Tess's phone in my lap. The browser has a bunch of screens open: one to her business email account, one to an account dedicated to fans, and a few to the various social media feeds she and Sammy have been hard at work updating during my little hiatus. I scroll through a few of the latest posts, where fans have added links to the story about Noel, my stomach lurching as I read the sleazy, over-the-top headlines. But the comments are more than just the usual heart emojis, exclamation points, and occasional trolls. Things like:

Hi Lily. First of all: I love u! Second, my dad has been in and out of jail and rehab my whole life and it sux. I hope ur friend's mom gets better. He's lucky 2 have u to talk to.

And:

I wish everyone would leave Noel's mom alone! She is trying to get better. I wish my mom would do that.

I pull up my latest Instagram post, a photo of Noel's arm, stretched over the edge of his boat, holding out a wriggling lobster. I'd captioned it: *Introducing: Dinner.* So far, it's been "liked" 1,176,006 times.

The most recent comment is from @lilylove02.

It says, simply: *Come home.*

28

30 Days Until Tour
August 13th

I CRUNCH UP the gravel driveway to Noel's house, relieved to find that neither his nor his dad's truck is parked out front. Though I've spent the last few days rehearsing all the many things I want to say to Noel, I'm really here to see Sidney.

The plan was to spend the whole day packing, since I leave for rehearsals tomorrow. But after roaming around the house, collecting stray flip-flops and sunglasses, and saying good-bye to the views from each window, I realized it was time. It's been four days since I last saw or heard from Noel, and I haven't stopped wondering what things have been like for him and his family. I've tried texting a few times, but when it became clear that he wanted to be left alone, I gave up. I wanted to apologize, but more than anything, I wanted to know how Sid was doing. I imagined her tearing down the postcards in her room, devastated.

Outside on the back deck, Sid has rigged up an impressive outdoor workspace situation, her laptop open on her lap and a towel thrown over her head and the screen to counteract the sun's afternoon glare. For the first time that I've seen all summer, she's wearing a bathing suit—a cute polka-dotted one-piece—and her legs and arms are oiled and glistening in the sun. I feel a tender tug near my heart, remembering her speech about the girls in her class and their blind dedication to summer tanning. I instantly remember, too, the peculiar loneliness of not being asked to do something you'd never want to do in the first place.

I put one foot on the uneven deck stairs and it groans beneath my weight. Sidney jumps, the towel crumpling into a heap between her head and her computer.

"Sorry," I say. "I was just . . . in the neighborhood."

Sidney looks at me skeptically. She folds the towel carefully and lays it on the deck beside her. "Does Noel know you're here?"

I shake my head. "He wouldn't return my calls."

Sid carefully snaps her laptop shut and hugs it to her chest. "He's been practically living on the water." She sighs. "He's pretty mad."

"I know," I say. "And I didn't want to bother you guys anymore, but I'm leaving tomorrow. I came to say good-bye."

Sidney hugs her computer and stares at her outstretched legs, her blond eyebrows pulled together. My heart is pounding in my chest and I have to bite the insides of my lips to keep from crying. I perch awkwardly across from her, my back to the crooked railing.

"Did you know that vitamin D deficiency causes cardiovascular disease?" Sid asks abruptly. "Also, asthma and cancer."

I stifle a surprised chuckle. "No," I say. "I didn't know that."

Sid nods seriously. "It can," she says. "That's why I'm out here. Not because I care about what the stupid girls in my class think."

"Okay," I say, braving a small smile. Sid nods again, picking at a sticker advertising the local public access station that is peeling from the corner of her laptop. "Sidney . . ." I start tentatively.

"I already knew," she says, looking up at me quickly. "About my mom, if that's what you're going to say. If you're here to, like, apologize to me for unearthing this terrible secret, or whatever, don't worry about it. I've known the whole time."

I stare at her, dumbfounded. "You have?"

Sid shrugs. "My dad worked so hard," she said. "It seemed like the highlight of his week. Going to the post office. Bringing me back those stupid postcards. You could see it in his eyes. There was this two- to three-minute window every time where I think he actually believed it himself. That she was somewhere incredible, seeing and painting beautiful things. That one day she'd just show up, all tan and happy, and things would go back to normal again."

There's a pressure in my jaw and I clench and unclench my teeth, trying to relieve it. "I'm sorry," I say. "I'm sorry to take that away from him. From all of you."

Sid looks at me. "You didn't take anything away," she says. "If anything, you gave us an excuse to stop lying, which is exactly what we needed. It wasn't healthy."

Sid drops her legs from the railing and picks up a bottle of sunscreen from the round patio table. She snaps open the lid and squeezes out a dollop of lotion into her hands.

"Something like forty percent of all heart attacks are caused by lying," she says, lathering her legs in solid white streaks. "Did you know that?"

This time, I can't help it: I laugh outright. "No," I say. "I didn't know that, either."

"That's because I made it up," she admits. "But still, it can't be good for you."

"You're right," I say. "You're right about a lot of stuff, you know that?"

Sidney shrugs again. "Not according to the people around here," she says, pressing the top of the lotion shut and laying it down on the table. "According to them I'm some kind of freak. Noel was so worried about what kids at school would think if they knew about Mom. That's the least of my problems. Half their parents are drunk most of the time, anyway." She shrugs. "Who knows, maybe now I'll finally fit in."

I drag one of the deck chairs closer to her and sit beside her. I want to do something ridiculous, like pick her up and put her in my pocket and keep her there until she's eighteen and old enough to go wherever she wants, be whoever she wants. "You know, I was just like you when I was your age," I say.

Sid gives me a sideways glance before dramatically rolling her eyes. I hold up my hand to keep her from interrupting. "I know. You probably think it's some ridiculous media invention or something I say to get publicity, and I wouldn't blame you if you did, but I promise it's the truth. I didn't have a lot of friends. I never had the right clothes, or cared about what anyone thought was cool."

Sid twists her rope bracelet, a twin of the ones she

gave to Noel and her father, around her wrist. "Really?" she asks, still not convinced.

"Really," I say. "And I know you probably have a lot of people telling you that things are going to get better, that someday you'll find your *tribe*, or whatever . . ."

As I'm talking I dig into my bag for my journal. I flip it open to a blank page and fumble around in the bottom of my bag for a pen.

"And I don't know if you will or not, but I do know that you're one of the strongest, smartest, and weirdest people I've ever met." I scrawl my phone number on a piece of paper and pass it over to her. "And if you ever find yourself looking for a tribe in the New York City area, give me a call."

Sid stares at the paper between her fingers. She looks from the number to me and back again. "I could do a lot of damage with this, you know."

"I know," I say. "And I'd deserve it."

"You would," Sid agrees, a stubborn smile pushing across her face. Before I know what's happening, she lunges for me, her long arms around my neck, her face pressed against my shoulder. I squeeze her tight, giving her ponytail a soft tug.

"What happened to your PDA-free zone?" A voice startles us.

Sid jumps back and we both turn to see Noel. He's in his orange waders, shiny rubber overalls tucked into big black boots, and he's hauling a trap down from the back of his truck.

I reach up to smooth my hair and fidget awkwardly with the hem of my shorts. Sid pulls me in for another hug. "If you need an out, remember: lady troubles," she whispers in my ear. "Like father, like son."

I give her a thumbs-up and walk toward the truck, where Noel is piling up the lobster pots on a dry patch of grass near the shed.

"Hi," I say, my hands clamped tightly behind my back. "Sorry. I thought you'd be out. I tried calling . . ."

"Yeah." Noel shrugs at the traps. "Dad wants to finish up the season strong. Says our numbers are low. Guess I've been slacking."

"That's probably my fault, huh?" I ask with a sad smile.

"Probably." He reaches into a cooler in the back of his truck and pulls out two bottles of water, offering me one. I take it and we stand together with our backs to the side of his truck.

I run my hand along a wide, shallow dent. "This was my fault, too," I muse, remembering the morning we met. What would this summer have been like if I hadn't gone into town that morning? If I'd stopped at the intersection as I was supposed to?

Noel leans over to peer at the damage and shrugs. "Add it to the list."

I glance down at the dirtied tops of my sneakers. As hard as I'm trying to fight them, hot tears push through the corners of my eyes. Standing here, with Noel, I wish we could just go back. I wish I'd never done that interview. I wish we could stay in our bubble, just the two of us, like the old man and his floating cabin, our own private island, forever.

"Hey," he says, nudging me gently. "I'm sorry. I shouldn't have . . . I didn't mean any of what I said. I was . . ."

I shake my head. "You were right."

"No," he says firmly. "I wasn't. I was mad. And scared. But it had nothing to do with you."

I look at him, the strong, square line of his jaw, his tired blue eyes. "I'm so sorry," I say. "If I had stopped and thought, I would never have been so careless."

Noel shakes his head. "I should have told you the truth."

"No," I say. "You shouldn't have. Not until you were ready. That's the problem. That's *my* problem. I try to do everything too fast. I never give things enough time to happen on their own. It's just . . . it's what I'm used to. It's the way my life works. I wish it wasn't, but it is."

"It doesn't have to be," Noel says. He turns the bottle

of water around in his hand, the plastic creaking and popping between his fingers. "You could stay."

I feel a fluttering in my chest. "Here?" I ask. "You'd still want me to?"

He looks at me carefully. "Of course," he says. "I've been thinking about it, and I don't think I can come away with you. Not now, anyway. I should be here. Sid, my dad . . . I owe it to them to stick around for a while."

I nod, imagining Sid and their dad battling with the microwave each night. I feel another pang and wish I could take them all with me.

"But you don't have to go," Noel continues, tentatively. "You could stay. Write more songs. When you're ready, you can leave for shows, tours, whatever. You don't have to give up your life. Just . . . slow it down a little."

I look out past his house, at the grassy hills, yellow-green and broken by stretches of blue. I breathe in the damp, salty air, like I'm trying to memorize the taste of it. All of it.

I twist my fingers inside Noel's rough palm. "I came here because I was trapped. Every relationship I've ever had ended badly and I thought that it was my fault, that there was something wrong with me. You showed me it wasn't true. I *can* be happy."

Noel squeezes my hand, an easy smile brightening across his face. The fluttering near my heart turns to a sharp ache. "I fell in love with you and this place at the same time," I continue. "You showed me a life I never thought I could have again—something grounded, and real. Something easy. You showed me how badly I want that." I take an uneven breath. "Someday."

I feel Noel's fingers loosen in mine. I feel him slipping away. "Someday?"

I nod reluctantly. "I'm sorry," I say. "I wish I could be ready now. But I'm not. There's more I need to do first."

"Can't you do it from here?"

"Not now," I say. "Being with you, your family, spending time away . . . it was just what I needed to see things differently. And seeing things differently helps me write the kind of songs that I should be writing. Songs about life—all of it, not just love songs. I need to be out there, experiencing more. If I stay . . ."

My mind wanders back to the morning Jed left, to sitting on the steps with Maya. I wanted everything to be easy, but maybe she was right. Maybe easy isn't the answer. There's a stirring inside of me that keeps me going, keeps me asking questions and writing songs to discover the answers.

"I know it probably sounds silly," I go on, feeling stronger now, "but I feel like I have this . . . one chance, you know? To say all of the things I want to say. And if some of it makes people feel better, or less alone . . . well, not everyone gets to do that. I don't know how long it will last. But I can't turn my back on it. On *them*. Not yet."

Noel crosses his arms in front of his chest. "So, what? I'm just supposed to wait here until the rest of the world is done with you? Until you're ready?"

My limbs feel suddenly restless, jittery. I want to wrap my arms around his waist and beg him to come with me. To convince him that his family will be fine, they don't need him. There's a whole world out there. He could be anyone. Do anything.

But I remember Maya again. Maya, Noel, they were born to speak the language of this place. It lives inside of them. They can leave and come back, but they'll always know what home feels like. They'll always feel that pull.

I don't have a home—not yet. But I know that pull. I know what it's like to feel incomplete without the rhythm of the road, the sound that forty thousand people make singing the same words, words that I've written. I think about Sidney, about the confused, quirky, sometimes-lost little girl I used to be. My songs are the way I've always made sense of the world, the mistakes I've made, the people I've met and what they've taught me. I'm not done with any of that. I don't know that I ever will be.

"Of course I don't expect you to wait," I say softly.

Noel tucks his chin low to his chest and stuffs his hands into his pockets. He kicks at the dirt driveway, dusty clouds rising up around our ankles. "But you still have to go?"

"I still have to go."

We stand quiet for a moment, beneath the faraway call of circling gulls, the roar of the ocean. One hand slides out of Noel's pocket and finds its way to mine. I rest my head on his shoulder and close my eyes, half of me wishing I'd never have to let go. Wishing I could keep this summer with me always, like a secret door I can duck inside whenever I need it. The summer I saw myself the way I used to be, before the bright lights and dark windows and forty thousand voices.

And half of me is already gone.

29

One Month Later
Los Angeles

"LILY?"

There's a quick knock on my dressing room before the door opens and Ray ushers in Tess and Sammy. He checks his watch and gives me *hurry-up* eyes while the distant, throbbing hum of an eager crowd vibrates in the walls around us. It's only been an hour since we finished sound check, but it seems like I've been backstage for a lifetime, staring vacantly at my heavily made-up reflection, listening to the insistent chanting, the echoes of my name tumbling into the room each time the door is opened.

"Li-ly! Li-ly! Li-ly!"

I shift to the edge of the L-shaped couch, tugging at

the tassels on my short sequined skirt. Tess and Sammy perch carefully on either side of me. I look back and forth between them and force a shaky smile.

"Any sign?" I ask, trying not to get my hopes up.

I watch in the mirror as they share a look. Sammy shakes her head. "The seats are still empty . . . Sorry, Bird."

I nod slowly. It's been weeks since Noel and I have spoken—we texted a bit in the beginning right after I left the island, but then things got too crazy, and it was easier, for both of us, I think, to make a clean break. Before we stopped talking, I sent him and Sidney tickets to the first show, but I never really believed they'd fly all the way out here. It's not that I'm surprised, but there's a part of me that has been holding out hope, and now the disappointment sinks in my gut like a stone.

"Nice digs." Tess glances around the swanky dressing room approvingly. It's the first time I've gotten ready for a show without them, and I know that's part of the reason I'm feeling so off.

"I think maybe this was a mistake," I say, as if there's still time to change my mind. As if I could duck out the side door and run back to the hotel without anybody noticing. Curl up with room service and an on-demand movie. The thought is so tempting it makes my whole body ache.

Sammy grabs my hand and squeezes it tight, while Tess shakes her head. Her hair has started to grow out, the short pieces underneath now feathery layers mixed in with the rest.

"You're just freaking out," she says flatly. She stands and pulls me to my feet, dragging me over to the mirror. "Look at yourself. You look . . ."

"I know," I say, grimacing at my shimmery leotard, the slinky skirt. "I look ridiculous."

Tess shakes her head, this time defiantly. She pushes me closer to the mirror. "You look *phenomenal*," Tess insists. "You look like a star."

"You do," Sammy echoes. "And it's okay to be nervous. But you're going to be great. Rehearsals have been going well, right?"

I scoff at my reflection. Rehearsals have been brutal. I've had to cram months' worth of new choreography and new set and costume changes into a handful of weeks. When I got back to the city, I was so out of shape that I could barely make it through an hour without collapsing. Lounging on a beach all summer didn't exactly prepare me to leap around onstage in high heels for twelve hours a day. And emotionally, I was a wreck—I was convinced I'd made a terrible mistake. I was distracted, and everyone knew it. Terry tried to mask his concern, but I could feel him watching me whenever I missed a step or fumbled a lyric, waiting for me to break down.

Then little by little, I snapped out of it. Learning the intricate steps, wearing the glittering costumes—it's been like a mini boot camp. I've had to relearn how to give myself over to something bigger than me, to the beautiful chaos of the tour machine, the theater of life on the road.

But there are still moments every day when it all comes back in flashes: when I see a guy with Noel's same broad shoulders working on set, hunched over a hammer, or when, running through lyrics, I remember the island, the life I could be living, the life I left behind.

"Bird, you've got this," Sammy says, as if reading my mind.

Tess holds out a hand. "Come on," she says. "Why would we lie? It's not like there's anything in it for us anymore." She winks at me and I follow nervously, the pulsing vibrations growing more intense as we near the door to the hall.

"Wait!" Sam calls out from behind us. She's bent over a side table, fiddling with her phone. When she straightens, the cheery introductory beat of our favorite preshow Madonna song blasts through a portable speaker.

"I can't believe we almost forgot." Tess grins. "You can't go onstage without a dance party warm-up."

Tess drops my hand and does a quick series of "Vogue"-inspired moves, beckoning me to join her. Sammy's arms are in the air, her face upturned as she shouts the lyrics at the ceiling. I laugh and feel the nerves settle into something closer to familiar anticipation and giddy excitement.

Something I can work with.

We dance and laugh until we're sweaty and out of breath, until Ray pokes his head in to tell us it's time.

My friends walk me to the wings and hug me tight, before ducking back to their seats on the other side. I watch them disappear and feel the stadium swelling around me. I squeeze my eyes shut and lose myself in the thousands of voices. There's a bustle of activity, people fussing with my hair, my clothes, pushing me into position beneath the stage, where I'll be shut into a glass elevator and lifted into view.

"Ready?" somebody on the crew asks. The machinery creaks and groans, the moving set is swallowed in darkness except for the streaks of light filtering through cracks overhead.

There's a whoosh inside of me, a great, sudden shift. Everything gets quiet.

It's just me. I know what I have to do.

"I'm ready," I say as the doors close around me and the floor starts to move, inching me up toward the light.

★ ★ ★

I stand onstage, my chest heaving, the final notes of a song echoing in the air. Lights swirl across the stadium in crisscrossing formation, shining back into the far reaches of the mezzanines, sweeping over hands and fingers and faces, tens of thousands of eyes on me.

I'm halfway through the first set, and my heart is racing, my cheeks sore from smiling nonstop. I'd forgotten this: that the first night of tour—after all the hard work of choreographing and rehearsing and planning and sound-checking—is always exhilarating. It's the pure joy of looking out at the sea of smiling, shouting, singing faces. Young faces, old faces, some in shy pairs and some in gleeful groups. Some faces are familiar, like my parents' in the front row, or Tess's and Sammy's, who, for the first time in years, are cheering in the audience and not frazzled and busy, hard at work backstage. It's a thrill like nothing I've felt before, a heart-blasting, blood-pumping energy in my veins, a bliss-filled balloon stretching between my ribs.

It's always been like this, the magic and euphoria I feel being back after a long break. But tonight, it's magnified and mixed with bittersweet relief. Sammy and Tess were right: Despite everything that's happened this summer, despite all my fears, I can still get up here and do what

I do. I can do it with everything that I have, everything that I've become. I can do it and still be me.

Now, as I stand onstage, the last chords fading around me and the deafening cheers dying down to a low rumble, I walk carefully to where the piano has been wheeled out. I told the crew I wanted to try something new tonight. After the opening, after I'd played a few favorites, I wanted to take a few minutes and just chat, as if I were sitting in my living room with a couple of friends. I'm pretty sure they all thought I'd lost it, but they humored me, and now the piano is here and the stadium is buzzing with a charged, expectant silence.

My stomach flip-flops and my pulse rages in my ears. Before I sit down, I lock eyes with Tess and Sammy. Their arms are linked and they're smiling like proud parents at a recital. I know I couldn't have done this without them. I also know that when the weekend is over, when the tour moves on and they head off to begin their own adventures, we'll all be just fine. We won't see each other as much, we'll have to work harder to keep in touch, but friends like these don't need titles, or daily check-ins, or routines. Friends like these are forever.

I sit at the piano bench, angling my crazy, impossible-to-walk-in lace-up stilettos toward the crowd. "Hi, guys," I say, adjusting my microphone's headpiece. The crowd explodes as if I've just given them all free cars. I giggle and hear my voice echoing overhead, wondering if I'll ever get used to this. I hope that I never do.

"I had an idea," I shout above the cheers. "It may be crazy, but I just want to . . . Would you mind if I talked to you for a minute? I promise I'll get back to the music soon, but there are a few things I want to say first. Is that cool?"

There's a roar and the lights come down, spotlighting me at the piano. I pull the bench in closer, leaning one elbow against the lid to get comfortable. I smile at the glow of tens of thousands of cell phones and cameras, each one like a tiny flame in a sea of shifting, silent bodies.

"First of all, thank you, from the bottom of my heart, for giving me the chance to disappear this summer," I say. "I'm going to be totally honest with you: I needed it. I was feeling . . . I was sad. And tired. And confused. And sometimes, when you're sad and tired and confused, you need to take a break. You need to hang out with the girls who knew you when you were a kid. You need to be that kid again. And that's what I did."

I find Tess and Sammy again in the darkness, the lights of the stage reflected in their smiling eyes. I take a deep breath.

"Also . . . I met someone this summer."

There's another, sudden roar, cheers and chants, and I see a few flapping signs that say things like: WHERE'S

NOEL? and WE LOVE NOEL! with giant hearts and arrows. I keep smiling, holding up my hands until the quiet returns.

"I know, I know," I say. "You wanted him to be here. I wanted him to be here, too. But sometimes . . . sometimes . . ."

The words falter. I'd had a whole speech planned, but now, sitting in front of thousands of hopeful faces, I've lost it. Being this honest about Noel is more difficult than I'd anticipated. I take a deep breath, trying to remind myself that this is the point. Not everything can be easy all of the time. Sometimes, the hard parts are what help us grow the most.

All night, I've been avoiding a certain section of the crowd, the seats I'd saved for Noel and Sid. But now I feel my eyes drawn there, as if my body needs a visual reminder. As if I need to remember the crazy love and the painful loss and the enduring heartache that pushed me to bare my soul here in the first place.

I steel myself and glance over the front rows, searching for the pair of empty seats . . . and then my stomach drops.

There, in the third row, are Noel and Sidney.

A sharp, piercing pain squeezes around my heart. The room starts to spin. I blink and look again. Sidney is standing on her seat, one arm resting on Noel's shoulder.

I can tell by Noel's posture that his hands are stuffed in his pockets. He looks sheepishly from side to side. Sidney waves one arm goofily over her head.

They're here. They came. My heart soars, a wide smile pushing across my face. But as soon as I turn back to the piano, a new and paralyzing fear creeps in. Here I am, about to do the same thing I've always done: share myself with thousands of strangers, invite them into my life in a way that might make some people uncomfortable. In a sense, it's the very thing that tore me and Noel apart. Is it worth it? Is it what I really want to do?

I look back at Noel, and our eyes lock. Beneath the uncertainty, beneath the fidgeting discomfort, I see him smile. And I know that he's okay. He'll be okay, and so will I. Which is funny, because that's just what I wanted to say tonight: Even if things don't work out exactly the way you'd hoped, even if it's not your perfect, happy ending, everything is going to be okay. Falling in love isn't everything.

It's a lot. But it's not everything.

I clear my throat and go on.

"Sometimes, life gives you all kinds of stuff at once, and you have to make choices. Sometimes what you want and what you need will be two different things. Sometimes life won't make sense, and things will be complicated, and it won't be easy. The choices won't be easy. But you're going to be okay. We're going to be okay. Because right here, right now, I choose all of you."

The stadium erupts and I stand up, now close to shouting, just to hear myself over the deafening roar. "*You* are the reason all my dreams have come true. *You* are the reason I get to do the thing I love most in the world every day and every night. I get to write songs, and we get to sing them together. So, as long as you show up, I'll show up, too. As long as you're here, I'll be here, too. Deal?"

There are whoops and shouts and I laugh, returning to the piano and pushing back the lid. I lay my hands on the keys, pressing into them slowly. I play the first few bars of "Let It Be," improvising until my fingers find the right, new chords.

"So this song is for all of you. It's for anyone who has a choice to make. Anyone who's still waiting. It's called 'Dear Sid,' and I wrote it for a very special friend of mine."

I sneak a glance at the crowd and see Sidney with her hands up to her face, her eyes wide and glistening.

I turn back to the piano.

I close my eyes and take a breath.

I sing.